A Duellist in Kansas

British Army officer John Carshalton is serving in Canada when he gets into a battle with a Frenchman over the affections of a girl. The dispute ends with Carshalton killing his love rival in an illegal duel and he must flee south of the border to escape court martial.

He finds himself in a small Kansas town near Abilene. There he stands with an ageing deputy sheriff against a group of outlaws and this earns him the respect and friendship of the town.

But the murdered Frenchman's brother is after him, intent on forcing John into one more duel. When this man teams up with the outlaws Carshalton originally faced, he finds his strong sense of honour and duty put to the test: he must face the danger he has unwittingly brought to his adopted town.

A Duellist in Kansas

Tom R. Wade

A Black Horse Western

ROBERT HALE · LONDON

© Tom R. Wade 2015
First published in Great Britain 2015

ISBN 978-0-7198-1620-8

Robert Hale Limited
Clerkenwell House
Clerkenwell Green
London EC1R 0HT

www.halebooks.com

Typeset by
Derek Doyle & Associates, Shaw Heath
Printed and bound in Great Britain by
CPI Antony Rowe, Chippenham and Eastbourne

ONE

'Don't look for trouble and trouble won't look for you.'

That was the advice that Josh had received from his father one day when only a child, standing on the bows of the Mississippi paddle steamer of which his father was the proud captain.

The advice might have carried more weight had not his father, deliriously relaxed one night on a bottle of 'Who Hit John?' destroyed every pier and jetty in Vicksburg, or so the story went.

Sacked by the steamboat company, he took to fur-trapping and took to it wholeheartedly, sporting a large fur coat that he so loved that he wore it winter and summer. He earned a rather disappointing Indian name of 'Man who Wears Fur Coat in the Winter and Summer.' This rather unimaginative if undeniably factual title was not well-known enough in the Indian nations to prevent a drunken Arapahoe from mistaking him for a grizzly bear and shooting him in the leg with an arrow. The wound festered and the leg had to be amputated.

Josh's father spent his remaining days playing the accordion badly on the deck of the very ship he had captained the length of the river.

Josh's life, if less colourful, had reflected his father's inability to stay out of trouble. He had spent much of his life in the army and it seemed that no conflict of any seriousness could occur without Josh being present.

Even when he left the army and became a lawman he seemed to attract, as he put it – 'like flies to horse shit' – every drunken cowboy with a grudge and a loaded gun.

One thing he had learned to do was not to trust strangers and tonight his life seemed full of them.

In these days of so much change there were always strangers. They came in every shape and size, moving west and south behind the railroad, on their way to step without care, all over the wounded animal that had been the Confederate South, stealing and being stolen from, blaming and being blamed, killing and being killed.

Some you noticed at once, some you just should have.

Josh would have been the first to admit he was not as observant as he used to be. He was slowing down, that much he also knew. When the rains started his bones ached and the scar left by a Confederate bayonet throbbed and pained. He could no longer sink into a chair without an involuntary grunt and he was forced to wear spectacles to read the handbills that arrived from Abilene and Wichita. But he still knew people and he knew to watch them closely.

So it was that Deputy Sheriff Josh Ramsey was sitting in his usual corner, giving as it did a view of the noisy, smoky, low-beamed bar of 'The Drover's Rest saloon and boarding House', or 'bawdy' house as the townsfolk liked to call it. In truth it was as tame as the town itself. Also true, it did boast two whores; Connie and Mary, but in reality they did little whoring and more waiting on tables, having their backsides fondled by the men too afraid of their wives to do anything but look and touch. The saloon was shabby, smelled of stale tobacco and bad food, but had a cosy, lived-in feeling that Josh felt unsettlingly familiar with.

Josh was watching strangers. He did not at that

moment need more strangers, so, as is the way, as he watched and sipped a warm beer, another stranger entered.

This man was out of place. He moved easily, almost arrogantly and he held himself well and tall, his clothes were cared for and the boots were expensive leather. Josh would lay good money he was a military man. He was handsome in a soft, boyish, round faced way. It made his age hard to place – perhaps late twenties. His skin looked pale but fresh, not leathered by prairie suns. He had a small scar on his left cheek, which was the only blemish that Josh could see. He spoke quietly when he ordered his beer but Josh had still been able to recognize the clipped tones of an Englishman. Not that it was unusual. A good number of them were part of the opportunists moving in the slow stream south and west, but this man was no carpetbagger.

Still, for the moment that stranger was not Josh's problem. It was an old familiar face and four new ones that were about to give him trouble. He had in fact broken his own rule. Not one but four strangers had entered the bar early and Josh had not seen them arrive. There were two who sat back in the shadows against the wall. Both men had thin sharp faces, men worn and old before their time, men

8

who, if Josh was any judge, had done prison time. Sitting on the other side of the table, nearer the thin light of the oil lamps was a man in his late thirties or early forties. A face that could have been handsome was spoiled by a thin scar that ran at an angle just missing his eye. He had a languid arrogance about him. Josh had learned to treat such men with caution.

However the real focus of Josh's attention was the youngest of the group. A young man with a cherubic complexion and an angry expression was in heated argument with Eb Hawkins. Eb was drunk, which came as no surprise to anyone, but this time he was drunk and mean, and that was unusual.

Eb had lost his wife and three children in California in '49 to claim-jumpers. He had tracked the men responsible eastwards and north to Kansas and killed them, and then, as so often happens when the hatred and the vengeance was gone, he realized he was left with nothing. Having reached Arabella he stopped moving and let the years and coarse rye whiskey dull the pain.

Tonight Eb was spoiling for a fight and when you feel that way, finding a likeminded person is never hard. Josh pushed forward through the crowd to join Eb at the bar.

Eb was already jabbing his finger belligerently into the chest of the young man. The boy had the look of a cowhand but he wore his gun holster strapped tight and had the nervous excited eyes of someone who thought he could use it. Josh suspected that he may not have used a gun to any great effect up to now but that did not make him any less dangerous.

'You don't like my tone, mister?' Eb stuck his pointed chin out in challenging fashion.

The young man's voice was hardening by the minute. 'No, I do not.'

'Well to you, sir, I say go straight to hell, because I will have just whatever tone I damn well please.'

'You poke your bony fingers in me just one more time and you will be waiting in hell for me.'

They were beginning to move apart, which meant trouble.

Josh moved in between them.

'Eb, you're drunk, drunker than usual. Now git. Go and sleep it off.'

'The hell I will. I had enough of these saddle bums who think they can come into our town and talk to us just as they goddam please.'

'Now just who are you calling saddle bums, you loud-mouthed old soak?'

This came from the languid man Josh had noted earlier. The two other men had also risen and were standing just behind him. Three more guns in total were now standing to the back of the younger man. Having missed their arrival Josh could easily surmise that these men had been in the bar a long time; natural meanness would have been well fuelled by the raw liquor of the Drover's Rest. A bad situation was about to get worse.

The young man spoke back over his shoulder 'I can handle this, Kyle.'

The older man smiled. 'I'm certain you can, Wills, but I'm just letting anybody else who might be interested know that you ain't alone.'

Josh tried an easy smile at the other men.

'He's drunk, boys . . . let's just let it be, eh?'

'And suppose we don't want to let it be?'

'I'm the law here, son. When I say let it be, I kind of mean that's what you are going to do.'

Just at that moment Josh felt his age. He felt, not for the first time lately, that this was a young man's work.

The man called Kyle spoke.

'Well it seems to me this is just a private matter, Deputy. Now why don't you just go about your business and let us talk it out with this gentleman here and I reckon we can bring him round to our way of thinking.'

Eb had gone quiet and was sobering fast, but he still had his hand on his gun.

Josh smiled again but he could feel the sweat beginning to form on his palms.

'Reckon I can't really do that seeing as it's my job to keep the peace in this town.'

Kyle sighed, a look of exaggerated regret on his face.

'Well that is a downright crying shame. Yes, sir, I will say that. That is a shame.'

It was about to happen, Josh let his hand fall near his gun. He tried to calculate the odds but it did not take much reckoning to work out that they were not good. He could move as he drew, that might throw the first shots off. At least one of them would shoot at Eb. Even so he tried to decide which one to take down first. Kyle looked the most confident, the most assured. He was probably the nearest thing there was to a leader. If Josh could take him it might throw the others but he doubted it.

The moment was now.

'It would appear to me,' said the soft voice somewhere out of his field of vision, 'that this is not precisely what I would term "fair play".'

It was almost in a comic slow motion that every head turned to stare at the young Englishman standing just to Josh's left.

'I understand perfectly that this is, of course, strictly speaking, a private matter. And normally I would not interfere in a private matter between' – he paused for a moment as though searching for the right word – 'gentlemen. But you see I was sitting trying to have a quiet drink and I am afraid you are disturbing me.'

Kyle recovered first.

'Mister, you are going to wish you had stayed having your quiet drink.'

He was reaching for his gun. That was the signal for them all to start to move. Their guns were only halfway from their holsters before they realized that things had changed yet again.

Nobody quite saw where the small pistol came from or quite how the Englishman had so quickly forced it into Kyle's mouth, but there Kyle was, bent slightly backwards over the bar with the barrel of the small handgun pressing towards the roof of his mouth.

'You will appreciate, sir,' the Englishman's tone had never changed from its quiet spoken insolence, 'that what we have now is a very difficult and vexing situation. The presence of your companions with all those guns makes me, as I am sure you will understand, apprehensive to the point where I might be described as being in a state of extreme nervous excitement.'

Josh could not help thinking that he had seen dead men closer to extreme nervous excitement.

'As a result,' the Englishman continued, 'I regret to say that whatever happens to me you are going to die. So tight is my finger on this trigger that at the first sensation of pain, the slightest contraction of a muscle, and your brain, such as I suspect it to be, will decorate the wall behind you. Unless, of course,' he said this almost as an afterthought 'it transpires that we can, between us, devise some solution.'

Kyle's eyes were as expressive as any man's Josh had ever seen. The cruel arrogance was gone. He was looking at death and he knew it. His hand moved slowly away from his gun, the fingers spread out, motioning gently towards the other men. They hesitated and eased their guns back into their holsters. The youngest man, Wills, was the last to do so and he did it with bad grace.

It was only at that moment that Josh realized that he had stopped breathing, and let his breath escape as softly as he could. He realized also that his own gun was still in its holster. He drew it gently.

'Unbuckle the gun belts, boys,' he said, desperately trying to keep his voice steady, 'drop them to the floor very, very gentle, then back out that door, get on your horses and ride out. Come back in the morning and you will get them back . . . empty.'

The youngest man looked set to protest.

'You can just take that, son, or leave it alone. I don't give one good damn which it is. If you prefer we can march right over to that jail and while you're over there as my guests perhaps I'll just get to wondering what four cowhands are doing here when the last drive went through two weeks ago. When I knows for a fact the next one is at least one hundred miles south. I might get to looking through my handbills to see if there is anybody I recognize.'

He looked straight at Kyle as he spoke.

'Harry,' he spoke over his shoulder to the barman, 'as soon as they are gone, I want you to close up. I want everybody out of here. I want that door locked, otherwise I am just likely to shoot the first person who steps in, armed or not.'

There was a moment before they did as he had instructed. There always was. Then, one by one, the gunbelts were thrown into a pile on the floor. Only

15

then did the Englishman remove his gun from Kyle's mouth. Kyle leaned forward, gagging slightly and rubbing his throat. Josh noted that the Englishman already had the other man's gun in his hand

They moved away slowly, determined to show their defiance. They passed through the swing doors and out into the night.

Amid much grumbling the other patrons downed their drinks and shuffled reluctantly out.

Harry swung the shutter doors closed and slid the bolt. The Englishman pushed his pistol back into the waistband of his pants and they all watched without comment as Eb Hawkins' knees buckled and he slid slowly to the floor.

Josh wiped his face with a neckerchief. 'I want to thank you for that. That was a bad fix I was in.'

'You had no choice. It is your job. I admire a sense of duty. That is why I intervened.'

'Son, I would like to buy you a drink.'

'That would be most appreciated, Sheriff. . . ?'

'Deputy Sheriff Ramsey, Josh Ramsey. And you are?'

Instinctively the Englishman stiffened and bowed slightly. 'John Carshalton. Your servant, sir.'

Josh smiled. 'I ain't got much use for a servant,

son, but I can always use another friend.'

The Englishman relaxed, smiled and bowed again. 'My pleasure.'

Josh ordered two beers and they took a table in the corner. Eb was at a table in the far corner, his head on his arms like a sleeping child. Josh was annoyed to find that his hand was still shaking as he filled and lit his clay pipe. He leaned back in his chair willing his body to relax. At last he fixed his eyes on the Englishman and spoke quietly.

'Now tell me, boy, would that be Leff'tenant or Captain Carshalton?

The young man frowned.

'It would be Captain.'

'I figured. OK, son, now I think it is time I heard your story.'

'With respect sir, it is a story I would prefer not to tell.'

'I never begrudge a man his privacy, Captain, and I know this don't seem hospitable after what you done for me tonight, but it's my job to know who is in my town . . . and why they're in my town. I ain't a judge, I'm just a tired old lawman trying to stay alive and keep other people alive. Besides, a true loner would have sat it out tonight. You stood up for someone you didn't know. Reckon that makes you someone who's got time for people. People like you aren't usually alone. So?'

Josh smiled at John and winked. The Englishman stared at him for a moment, then something within him relaxed. He took a pull at his beer and nodded.

Harry had left them the keys and retired to his room above the bar looking a relieved man. And so they talked.

John Frederick Carshalton was born the only son of a rich milliner in a fine stately house in Northumberland, England.

His father, although a stern and hardnosed businessman, was nevertheless indulgent of his pretty wife, many years his junior, and was willing to please her by being equally indulgent of their only son.

Young John wanted for nothing and could easily have grown spoiled and lazy, but for two things; his mother's ability to lavish love, kindness and discipline in equal measures, and his own tendency to seek danger and endure hardship as though rebelling against all the luxury that was his to have.

Also he inherited from both parents a fine competitive spirit. John, from the beginning, had to climb highest up the tree, swim further out, ride his horse faster, and when circumstances demanded, punch harder.

Money bought John into one of the best schools in the North of England. There he rose above the natural prejudice of the English upper class against people like his father; whom they sneeringly called 'trade'; displaying their peculiar prejudice against money earned as opposed to money inherited. John used all the charm and daring he had inherited from his mother to win friends and beat enemies. His progress to head boy seemed almost ordained.

His father's dream of his son taking over the family business was dashed when John announced he wished to join the army. Again his father dug deep in his purse to pay the £7000 needed to secure a commission and place his son at the Royal Military Academy at Woolwich.

John took to the army, as everybody who knew him expected he would and when Lieutenant John Carshalton stepped out into the world of service to his Queen and country he found himself shipped away to Canada, and there for the first time, young John failed to shine.

The reason he failed to shine was that there was nothing to shine at. In 1870 Britain's military presence was fast coming to an end. A Canadian militia was being formed and the role of the British was that of advisors. John's meteoric rise came to an abrupt and frustrating end.

Day after monotonous day he polished equipment, cleaned his uniform, drilled the disconsolate rabble that he commanded and dreamed of great military actions and daring do.

The only small comfort was the pleasant society around him, among whom he enjoyed a round of balls and dinners and high teas, and no member of that society was pleasanter than Marianne Matrait.

At this, Josh raised his eyes from the bowl of his pipe that he had focused on through John's entire story. John caught his eye and smiled, almost apologetically.

'It involved a young lady.'

'It so often does, son.'

'It is indeed, I am afraid, a rather familiar situation but nonetheless real for that. We met at a regimental dinner for the local dignitaries. We arranged to meet again. We fell in love. Her name is Marianne, the daughter of a local industrialist. I courted her; I showed her and her family the respect you would expect an officer of the Queen to show.'

Fresh on the heels of this good fortune fate shone again on Lieutenant Carshalton, in the form of a man called Louis Reil, who led a rebel band of French half-breeds against the Dominion Government in the state of Manitoba. He succeeded in taking and occupying Fort Garry and subjecting the surrounding community to oppression and loss of their possessions. It all culminated in the murder of a young man named Thomas Scott. This last brutal act was enough to warrant a force being raised against Reil. It consisted of Canadian Militia from the First Ontario Rifles and the men of the Second Quebec Rifles under the command of Garnet J Wolsely, and officers of the 60th Royal Rifles including, of course, Lieutenant Carshalton.

John's dreams of glory in battle were dashed however when the closest they got to the enemy was a glimpse of the heels of fleeing rebels as the force approached Fort Garry.

Nonetheless, Lieutenant Carshalton was adjudged to have acquitted himself well and had won the respect of his men. This and an outbreak of cholera that thinned the ranks of officers and men led to a promotion to a captaincy. This time, the system of purchasing commissions having just been abolished, his long suffering father did not have to dig any deeper into the Carshalton purse to finance it.

Promotion, of course, increased John's eligibility in the eyes of Marianne's family and early talk of an engagement began. Then Jean Cottin arrived on the scene.

Josh had seen this coming.

'Something tells me, boy, you didn't have the stage all to yourself.'

'As you surmise, there was a rival for her affections. A Frenchman named Cottin, Jean Cottin. He pressed his own suit. . . .'

Josh looked up from the latest attempt to keep his pipe smoking with a puzzled expression.

'He did what?'

'He made advances.'

'Ah.'

'Unwanted advances; it was not the lady's wish. However, he was an important business associate of her father so her family permitted this. He contrived every means at his disposal to provoke me. Eventually he claimed that my advances were an insult to the lady and he challenged me to give him satisfaction on the field of honour.'

'That sounds like a hell of a fancy way of saying he called you out, boy.'

'He knew that, as a gentleman, I could not refuse.'

'The hell! You can always refuse. Tell him to go and satisfy himself.'

Josh impressed himself with his own unintentional vulgarity, and had to suppress a chuckle as John continued to pour out his heart.

'It was a matter of honour.'

Josh snorted, 'Honour? I'll tell you, John, I followed William Tecumseh Sherman all the way down the Shenandoah Valley and on to the sea. I saw a lot of men die, and I did some of the killing, but I didn't see one lick of honour in any of it.'

'Josh, I too am a soldier.' John paused to correct himself. 'Was a soldier. You cannot compare the field of battle to a dispute between gentlemen.'

'Killing is killing, son, and if there is any way to avoid it, then my advice is, do just that.'

'Nonetheless, I did not avoid it. We settled the matter and the man is dead. It was not, in fact, my intention to kill him. I am a good shot. I meant simply to wound him. But, there we are. Unfortunately, duelling is no longer permitted in Her Majesty's Army and I would have had to face a court martial.'

'If it was against regulations then there was your

good God-given reason not to do it.'

'It was.'

'A matter of honour. I hear you. Go on.'

After the duel, John had crossed the Canadian border and found his way to Boston. There he had sold his sabre and his medals. He had not however sold his horse or his uniform. With the horse in a boxcar he had travelled as far as Abilene. From there he had sent a letter to Marianne.

Then he had saddled Pilot and set off with no clear idea of where he was going or what he would do when he got there.

Josh disappeared in a cloud of smoke as he enjoyed a moment of rare success with the pipe. When he emerged he was staring thoughtfully at John.

'Son, I haven't known you long and in that short time you have saved my life, so you will have to forgive me for what I am about to say. You have managed to kill a man you truly had no desire to kill; you have been forced to run from a job that you love, and from a girl that you love. It is my considered opinion, boy, that you have behaved like a horse's ass.'

John Carshalton poured the remains of his beer down his throat. He took a small handkerchief from his pocket and wiped his mouth, and then he leaned back in his chair and sighed.

'It is my considered opinion, sir, that you are indisputably correct.'

TWO

De Saille was enjoying the pain he was inflicting.

The young whore was bent backwards over the bed. She was shaking with terror. Her eyes were wide; the nightdress had fallen away from her small breasts. De Saille was running the long thin blade of the knife around the small pink nipples.

'The problem is, little one, that you do not please me.'

He said it in a flat, almost matter-of-fact way. The coldness in his voice caused the young girt to shake even more.

The problem that De Saille faced was that he did not know what to do next. Now that the initial cold thrill of his rage had subsided to simply a dull throbbing anger he had to make a decision. The simple truth was that it was De Saille who had failed in the act of love, De Saille who could not relieve his natural cruelty through his usual savage thrusting.

De Saille should have been a handsome man; he was tall and slim with a fine head of black hair that fell to his shoulders, but for some reason he was not. Possibly the cold cruelty in the eyes froze the rest of the face.

Whilst he hated the whore for failing to excite him, he knew that he could not beat her as he wished to beat her for fear that his failure would be broadcast throughout New Orleans to amuse his many enemies. He certainly could not kill her. Whores were valuable to Blind French Francine, the colourfully named madame of this sordidly elegant whorehouse. Francine was neither blind nor French but pretended, when she wished to impress certain clients, to be both. Neither indeed was her name Francine, but she was the kind of woman that most people decided could be called anything she god-dammed pleased. She was a brutally hard Scot who had learned her trade in the back streets of Glasgow. She hated all men with cold, almost clinical intensity, but she hated De Saille even more.

However, he spent money lavishly on her whores and her expensive brandy so she tolerated him. Still, De Saille knew that if he damaged any of what

Francine called 'my stock' she would make it her pleasant duty to see a rope round his neck.

He was saved from making any decision at all by a knocking at the door, and the voice of Francine.

'De Saille, you have a visitor.'

'Who is it?'

'His name is Andre Cottin. I think he has business for you.'

For you, not with you, that was interesting.

'You "think"?'

'Far as my French goes, De Saille.'

'Tell him I will be with him shortly.'

Such was Francine's contempt for De Saille that she never bothered to maintain the phoney French accent when she addressed him.

'Tell him yourself, I'm not your serving lass, and if you are raising a hand to one of my best whores I'll cut that limp pecker of youse off and make you wear it round your neck.'

She stomped off, leaving De Saille scowling at the closed door. He turned back to the girl shivering on the bed.

'We have unfinished business, little one. Oh yes, in more ways than one we have unfinished business.'

He pushed the knife into the top of the tall

leather boots he wore and rose from the bed. As he rose he struck her. He did it with the sweep of one arm, contemptuously as one would swat an insect. The girl rolled off the bed and fell heavily to the floor, where she lay sobbing.

De Saille found his visitor in the main parlour, sipping a brandy and watching the carriages rattle past in the street outside. He rose to greet De Saille as he approached, took his hand and bowed stiffly from the waist.

'Monsieur De Saille? My name is Andre Cottin. I am pleased to make your acquaintance.'

The greeting was indeed in French and De Saille realized that he was surprised. It was so rare now to hear or speak his native tongue in this part of New Orleans.

'*Enchanté, Monsieur.*'

Cottin indicated the seat opposite him. 'The brandy here is surprisingly good. May I offer you a glass?'

De Saille shook his head. 'I have made my living from having a steady hand.'

In fact, De Saille enjoyed brandy rather too much, but it also seemed prudent not to admit this to a prospective client.

Cottin smiled and raised his glass in salute.

29

'Then, sir, you bring me to the point of my visit. I wish to hire your services.'

De Saille was taking a few moments to study the other man. He was short, smartly dressed, and dapper in fact, as only small men can be. He had a neat moustache that seemed too big for the small face. He sat relaxed but upright with one leg carefully folded over the other; self-consciously he smoothed one leg of his breeches at regular intervals.

De Saille felt no need to say anything at this stage. He simply let his large frame slump in the chair and listened.

'I want you to help me kill someone.'

De Saille raised his eyebrows just slightly. Here was a man who was choosing his words very carefully.

'I could, of course, simply pay you to kill him. Your reputation suggests that you are perfectly capable.'

De Saille allowed himself a smile and a slight bow of the head.

'However, I need to kill this man myself. It is a matter of honour.'

De Saille's smile faded to a frown. There was, in his experience, only one way to kill a man, and that was in the fastest most effective way possible. There was seldom much honour in it. De Saille had hoped that here in America such stupidity had been left behind in the salons of Paris.

'The man in question may have friends. I need to ensure that I am not interrupted in any way. You understand my meaning, I trust?'

Oh yes, De Saille thought, I deal with half a dozen bodyguards while you stand in the dawn light and say prayers and shake hands with your enemy. How wonderfully civilized for you.

He said, 'Who is this man?'

'An Englishman.'

'Ah.' De Saille allowed himself another smile. 'In that case you do add an element of pleasure.'

Cottin sipped delicately at his brandy.

'Yes, I was led to understand that you had no love for the English. Not since they forced you out of Canada.'

'You seem to know a great deal about me, sir.' De Saille could not disguise the annoyance in his voice.

'Take it as a compliment, sir. This matter is very important to me. I want the best. Everything I have heard tells me you are the right man.'

'May I ask what your grievance is with this man?'

Cottin looked genuinely surprised.

'Does it matter to you?'

De Saille shrugged. 'Ordinarily no . . . but I work alone. If I am to . . .' He paused to choose his words, 'assist you, I would prefer to know the nature of the business.'

Cottin smiled again. 'But of course. The Englishman's name is John Carsholton. Captain John Carsholten of the British Army.'

De Saille looked uneasy for the first time. 'Killing soldiers can sometimes cause, shall we say, upset?'

'Not if they are deserters.'

'That does indeed pose less of a problem.'

'John Carsholton killed my brother Jean in a duel six months ago in Canada. The British army is typically squeamish about such things. Duels have been banned for over thirty years. Carsholton faced the prospect of a court martial and disgrace. He chose to run.'

'You say he killed your brother in a duel. Personally, I have never seen killing as a chivalrous art form, but my understanding is that provided the duel was properly conducted the matter must be considered to be closed.'

'In most cases, yes. However, I believe that Carsholton behaved disgracefully in a matter over a lady. He gave my brother no choice but to challenge him to preserve her honour even though he knew Carsholton to be a far superior shot. I feel therefore that in this case justice has not been served and it is my intention to right a considerable wrong.'

De Saille sighed. Nothing that he was hearing suggested that this was a man he wanted to ride with, and even less go with into what was clearly going to be a difficult situation. De Saille had always considered idealists to be dangerous men. They were the sort who believed that war is some sort of game, that there can actually be any honour or dignity about violent death. That it was all anything other than blood and pain and darkness.

He brought his thoughts back to what Cottin was saying.

'I understand your reservations, Monsieur De Saille. You are a professional. You have a different attitude to such matters. However, I am, I can assure you, a rich man. I will make this work extremely profitable for you.'

'You interest me, of course, but I have to know more about the situation. Do we know where this man Carsholton is?'

'My sources tell me he is in Kansas, in a town called Arabella, twenty miles from Abilene.'

'They have law in Kansas these days. Lawmen

who may not take any more kindly to duels than the British Army does.'

'Then I probably will not bother to ask the permission of the law. This is a small town with one deputy sheriff. It is he whom Carsholton has befriended. The county marshal will be many miles away when we transact our business.'

'So the Englishman has only one other gun with him?'

'To the best of my knowledge.'

Yes, De Saille thought ruefully but it is one other gun that may not stand and wait for a handkerchief to be dropped. A little too vulgar for you, eh *monsieur*?

De Saille forced a smile. 'Then I do not anticipate any great problems.'

'Splendid, then I can take it your answer is yes? Excellent. In that case I will drink...alone...to the success of this venture. To an honourable conclusion, *monsieur*.'

THREE

It was at Tremaine, a small but growing town on the Kansas/Missouri border that things changed.

Had it not been for the events in Tremaine that hot afternoon Noel De Saille and Andre Cottin would have arrived in Arabella to find themselves outnumbered and unable to continue the matter of honour so dear to Cottin. They would have had their weapons removed. They would have been arrested and taken to Abilene. There they would have been put on the train and returned to New Orleans, where De Saille would have been paid and wryly seen the humour of the whole situation. Cottin would have sulked back to Canada denouncing the Englishman as a coward and vowing to seek his revenge again, one day.

He would probably have grown old still uttering

such threats.

It was not to be.

In Tremaine De Saille and Cottin were about to meet men who had their own personal score to settle with a young Englishman who had humiliated them, who had pushed a gun into the mouth of one, and who had been cool and arrogant. They would meet them in a way that the citizens of Tremaine would remember for a long time.

As De Saille and Cottin stepped down from the train, four men were about to ride into town. Only three of these men would ride out.

It was a hot, lazy day in a small town that was beginning to grow and was enjoying the feel of it. The coming of the railway had changed the fortunes of Tremaine. The church and the school were built. The hotel had been bought by a couple from back East who understood the business and were busy turning it into the kind of place respectable business men liked to stay. A new store seemed to open every month and rumour had it that a large granary company was enquiring about land.

Tremaine had a gentle bustle to it that afternoon. Nothing too fast, nothing too pushy, just a sense of purpose; a sense of getting there.

De Saille and Cottin intended to spend a night in

the hotel, after enjoying a bath and a meal, then to purchase horses and ride west to Arabella.

They deposited their bags but were forced to wait while the courteous but firm proprietor insisted that their rooms were not yet ready.

They crossed the dusty street to the saloon and were sitting on a bench outside sipping beer and watching the town busy itself when Kyle and Wills rode by.

At once De Saille could see that these men were out of place. They might have been drovers, once but no longer. They did not carry the trail dust of weeks in the saddle. They did not have the carefree look and wild exuberance of men who had tasted a cold beer in their minds for days. They did not look to left or right. They wished to make eye contact with nobody. They moved slowly on their horses, gently pulling on the reins, easing them back.

De Saille had, until then, been lost in his own thoughts. He had, as he suspected, little in common with Cottin, who was a prim and depressingly earnest companion and who took himself relentlessly seriously. His conversation consisted of chronicling his business ventures and bemoaning his distance from Paris.

Now De Saille began to look about him for

something that might be of interest to these two horsemen. It did not take him long to find it.

A few hundred yards down the street was the town's bank. It was about to close and a tired and hot clerk was courteously ushering the last persistent customers out.

The two men dismounted and let their horses drink from the long trough near the hardware store, but De Saille noticed that their eyes were following the movements at the bank.

Kyle and Wills were indeed watching events at the bank closely. They had all watched it on several occasions over the last week. They knew the routine. In the next five minutes the manager and three clerks would leave having locked the old and extremely vulnerable wooden vault. The manager, Cecil Hardwick, knew it to be old and vulnerable, and had hinted as much to Kyle, who had visited three days previously in his best 'going to chapel' breeches and top coat to express an interest in setting up a gunsmith business in the town and opening an account.

Cecil had noticed the look of surprise on Kyle's face at the sight of the vault, and had immediately interpreted this as deep concern. He had been quick to assure this obvious entrepreneur that a brand new vault of the very strongest iron and steel was due to be delivered in only three short weeks.

Armed with this information Kyle understood two things; the bank was a pushover and that they had better move quickly.

They watched now as the staff left locking the door and wishing a good evening to Jack Tanner. Tanner was the security guard whose duty it would now be to patrol outside the bank until relieved by a sheriff's deputy at midnight. Tanner carried a handgun and a shotgun and with neither, according to popular wisdom, could he 'hit a barn if he was standing inside it'. However, Cecil Hardwick was a careful man and was not about to lavish the bank's profits on employing the kind of expensive eastern agencies his colleagues preferred.

Tanner sat himself in the rickety wooden chair on the porch of the bank in a position that gave him a good view the length of Main Street. The strategic advantage of this would be seriously curtailed in the next thirty minutes when the warm evening sun would, as it always did, lull Tanner to sleep.

Tanner had only been settled for a few moments when Penny and Jones rode in from the other side of town on a wagon. On the back of the wagon was a large barrel. As they moved out of the side street and began to move slowly in front of the bank, Wills swung into the saddle and began to move towards them. Kyle also climbed into the saddle and moved off down to the opposite side of the street.

De Saille continued to watch with growing fascination as the little drama unfolded. Beside him Cottin grumbled about the heat, the dust, the smells, and the ugliness of the west.

As the wagon passed the front door of the bank, Wills spurred his horse forward and appeared to collide with the two horses pulling it. All three horses reared; the two in the shafts only able to rise slightly against the restraints of the harness. Wills and Jones started swearing and uttering threats at the tops of their voices. Penny seemed to be struggling to control his horses and the wagon was beginning to back towards the door of the bank. Looking closely, De Saille could see that Penny was pulling back on the reins and Wills was pushing forward with his own horse, driving the wagon up on to the porch of the bank and towards the doors.

Tanner, unsure what to do, had propped his shotgun against the wall and was on his feet watching the action. Townspeople were beginning to gather too, some shouting advice to Penny, others counselling calm between Wills and Jones. In a matter of moments, the quiet of late afternoon had been turned into a circus.

The rear of the wagon crept its way up the two short steps, wooden planks splintering beneath it until it struck the doors of the bank with a thud. There was a further tearing of wood as the hinges partly gave way. The barrel, large and heavy, being full of sand and stones, toppled with some assistance from Jones, and rolled the length of the wagon. It smashed into the already damaged door and tore it from its hinges.

By now, several more things were happening. Sheriff Nathaniel Coogan had, until a few moments before been contentedly filing arrest reports, of which there were happily few, when he was attracted by the commotion.

An ex-US cavalry major, he was a tall, smartly dressed man with a neatly trimmed moustache and stiff upright bearing that befitted a much-decorated officer. He rose from his chair, donned his smart black hat and paused briefly as he always did to check his appearance, not from vanity but from a dread of not cutting the correct figure of authority when he stepped out on to the streets.

He walked slowly towards the scene and, being an altogether quicker thinker than Tanner, realized

41

what was happening. He broke into a run, reaching for his revolver as he did so. Kyle, ambling several paces behind, spurred his horse into a gallop and drawing his own gun struck Coogan neatly behind the right ear with the butt as he passed. Coogan pitched face down in the dust as Kyle reached the bank.

Kyle took a stick of dynamite from his saddle-bag and handed this to Penny. Penny, who had learned how to handle dynamite during an uncharacteristic spell of honest work in mining, knew exactly what to do.

He stepped across the back of the wagon and into the bank, kicking the shattered door to one side as he did so. He lit the short fuse and deftly jammed the explosive against the rusty lock of the inappropriately named strong room.

As he left the bank at speed Wills, Jones and Kyle were already pulling the wagon round to the side of the bank, hurriedly releasing the horses from between the shafts.

Tanner was desperately trying to understand all that was happening. He was torn between a sense of duty and going for his shotgun, and a sense of preservation and turning and running. In the event he did neither. The dynamite exploded as he stood there, showering him with broken glass and blowing him backwards over the handrail of the front porch, on to the street, where he lay groaning and covered in blood. In fact it proved later that his injuries consisted mainly of cuts and bruises and a perforated eardrum. He would live to tell the tale, and indeed retell it a great number of times. As one wearied listener was to observe, 'Tanner went deaf and the rest of the town just wished they had.'

The onlookers to the initial drama had, on seeing the dynamite produced, scattered in panic. Indeed it was amazing how quickly a street could empty. However, Kyle and Wills faced down the main street with their guns drawn as Jones and Penny worked in the smoke-filled strong room, stuffing banknotes into two saddle-bags, their eyes and noses streaming from the smoke and fumes.

The other two people still on the street were De Saille and Cottin. Cottin had jumped to his feet as the raid commenced but De Saille had pulled him down. Now the pair sat quietly watching the action. Kyle watched them for a moment and wondered if they were about to interfere. He decided not.

Beside him Wills was in constant movement, spinning on his heel waving his gun back and forth, sweeping the empty street. Kyle himself felt strangely calm, in control; it was working, it was going well. He called back over his shoulder.

'Make haste, boys.'

Penny and Jones emerged, blinking in the sunlight. The two saddle-bags were full to overflowing. Jones jerked his head back.

'There's more.'

'That's plenty. Go now, boys, go.'

Jones and Penny each threw a saddle-bag over their horse's neck and swung into the saddle. They spurred their horses to a gallop, heading straight off down Main Street. Kyle and Wills also mounted up, each wheeling his horse, moving off in opposite directions, heading for side roads out of town.

It was at this point that the otherwise flawless operation went wrong. For the reason that all such men as Kyle fear and cannot ever guard against; the onlooker who refuses to run.

The onlooker in this case was Abraham Bartlett. A man who had fought his way through the Civil War for the Confederate army and was not about to watch his town being robbed by a gang of what Abraham firmly suspected was 'damned Yankee cutthroats'.

He took his Springfield breech-loading rifle, a trophy from a dead Yankee soldier, and stepped out from a side alley as Penny and Jones thundered down towards him. He shouldered the rifle and fired his first shot.

It was devastating. The bullet hit Penny in the chest, driving through his heart, killing him. The force of the shot against his speeding horse had the effect of snatching his body back off the beast into the path of Jones, whose own horse swerved, then reared and kicked in terror. Jones saddle-bag fell from the horse into the dust to join that of Penny's, who had taken it back with him as he fell.

It took Jones several yards to bring his horse under control and he was attempting to wheel it round to retrieve the saddle bags as Kyle, who had spun round at the sound of the shot, shouted, back at him.

'Leave them. I'll get them.'

Jones did not need telling twice. He dug his heels deep into the horse's flanks to drive it as far from the old madman with the gun as possible.

Kyle galloped forward, drawing his revolver for the second time that afternoon. This time, however, he meant to kill the crazy old man who was at that moment standing in the street readying himself for another shot.

Kyle fired two shots as he came but both missed.

The old man swung the rifle back up to his shoulder and fired again, but the approaching outlaw had unnerved him; he snapped at the shot and missed.

He did not however, miss by much, and the shot caused Kyle's horse to buck and rear, throwing Kyle on to the ground. He hit the ground hard; the force drove the air out of his lungs and sent his gun spinning away under the sidewalk. The terrified horse kept going and galloped off down the street.

Kyle was only a few feet from where De Saille and Cottin had been sitting. Cottin, in a state of great agitation, had risen from his chair and was pressed back against the wall, fearful of stray shots. De Saille, by contrast, continued to lounge in his chair with an air of arrogant amusement at the whole scene. In fact, whilst he felt no great fear, knowing as he did that the players in this particular drama had no time to concern themselves with the audience, he was fascinated and thrilled by what he was witnessing. The tedium of the trip had suddenly been forgotten, he was enjoying himself enormously.

Kyle had struggled to his knees and was attempting to breathe normally as old Abraham approached him, determined to put an end to the matter.

De Saille contemplated the scene before him for a moment, and felt that he would have preferred a different result. De Saille felt that the robbery had been rather well planned and executed. Had it not been for the intervention of this foolish old man it would, in fact, have been carried out without anyone getting seriously hurt. It was therefore, De Saille reasoned, the fault of the old man with the rifle and not the man in the dust.

At that point, De Saille considered that the odds needed to be a little more even. Beneath his coat, he slid his revolver from the holster on his hip and helped it to slide down the side of his leg so that it came to rest on the wooden boards of the sidewalk without a sound. Placing his right foot against the gun he flicked with the toe of his boot, sending it flying out off the sidewalk to land in front of Kyle.

Whether it was this movement that distracted Abraham could never be known but what is certain is that for a moment he hesitated. In that moment Kyle, without time to think where this particular gift had come from, grabbed the gun and moved it in a sharp upward arc firing as it went.

Three shots hit Abraham. One in the stomach, one in the chest and the other smashed through his cheekbone at an upward angle blowing out part of

47

his brain as it burst from his skull.

Abraham Bartlett, pioneer, prospector, decorated for gallantry by the Confederate army at Shiloh, was dead before his old face, leathered by sun and wind, drove into the dust of Main Street.

To Kyle, adrenaline pumping through him, it all appeared to be happening in slow motion, and in the same slow motion he saw Wills riding from the bank end of Main Street towards him. As he approached he slowed and leaned down towards Kyle. Kyle gripped Wills at the crook of his elbow and let the momentum of the horse carry him on to its back behind Wills. Surprised by the additional passenger the horse shied, and in that moment Kyle looked in the direction from which the gun had come.

He stared directly into the eyes of De Saille. Kyle's own eyes were full of questions. De Saille merely smiled slightly and bowed his head.

The horse regained its composure and its pace. It galloped to the end of the street and out across the open spaces beyond.

For a moment an awful stillness and silence descended on Main Street and then, as though at some unheard command, the townspeople began pouring from their various shelters to converge on the scene.

Some were helping Tanner, who was bleeding from the ears and moaning quietly. Others were helping Sheriff Coogan to his feet. Coogan was staggering and trying desperately not to vomit as waves of pain went through his skull and the world spun in a confusion of light and noise.

Others gathered round old Abraham. There were screams of horror from women and curses from men.

One old friend of Abraham's, who had known him since their army days, sat down in the dust beside him, tears streaming down his face.

'Will you look at this, will you look at this, if you please? Shot to bits, God dammit, shot him in the face. God damn their eyes.'

Somebody else was kneeling and reciting the Lord's Prayer.

A smaller crowd gathered around the body of Penny. Somebody kicked at it, someone else spat on it. By the next day the body would be embalmed and lying in an open coffin, leaning upright against the wall of the bank, with many of the citizens of Tremaine posing for photographs beside it in the hope that posterity would take them for heroes.

Unseen in the general confusion, De Saille got up from his chair and walked to the edge of the sidewalk. Still unseen he bent and picked up Kyle's pistol which was lying half under the wooden boards. One of the crowd turned towards De Saille and Cottin.

'You two there, you were close. Did you get a good look at them? Would you know them again?'

'Oh yes,' De Saille smiled faintly, 'I would, but I think it very unlikely I will ever see any of them again.'

FOUR

Josh always said that as you approached Arabella, riding from Abilene, the town looked like a lazy dog lying in the hot sun. He never managed to find a suitable image to describe what it looked like in the driving rain, or the dust storms, or the 'twisters' that blew in with little warning, but for a man of small imagination, it was not bad.

Arabella, lying between Abilene and Wichita, was a straggling mixture of the sod-built dwellings of the early settlers and new timber-frame buildings such as the jailhouse, the saloon and the general store.

The town had lost the first battle to share in the growth of the West. It had got it wrong and it knew it.

It had hoped to service the cattle drives coming up from Texas using the extended Chisholrn Trail,

51

but it had placed itself too close to Abilene. The trail-weary cowboys just wanted to press on, to get the longhorns sold and go home.

Then the railway was going to be its saviour, but the railway never came. The land immediately to the south had proved too difficult to cross. Instead the surveyors had found a better route to the west, just close enough for the townsfolk of Arabella to hear the whistle blow in the distance, like a mocking laugh, ridiculing their ambitions.

So they made do with the occasional drives too low on provisions to make Abilene, drifters and the constant trickle of immigrants heading west for greater riches. But they endured, and the farm-steads were slowly growing in the face of the twisters and the dust storms, and children were being born. Slow and painful though it was, a future was being built.

It was a pace that suited Josh well. He had had a hard life in many ways and his time in the uniform of the Union army had left both physical and mental scars. He wanted as much as possible to have a quiet life, and, other than the occasional incident like the one involving Eb, he managed it.

It had been a month since that night in the saloon when he thought that finally his luck would run out. The four men had not returned for their guns, which had made Josh suspicious. He had searched the handbills and come up with likenesses for three of them.

They were Kyle Banner, wanted in Waco for robbery and wounding; Silas Jones, wanted in Oregon and Texas for robbery and cattle rustling, and Charles Penny, wanted in Wyoming for bank robbery. As he suspected, both Jones and Penny had seen the inside of prisons, although in Penny's case it had been as a Confederate prisoner of war at Johnson's Island. He had nothing on the younger man, Wills, but it was early in his career and Josh had little doubt that literature would soon be forthcoming.

However, the men appeared to have disappeared from the area and therefore were no longer of any concern to Josh. He put them from his mind and concentrated on the day to day chores of keeping peace in Arabella.

The young Englishman had settled in the town. He had found employment of a sort, helping Wolfgang Kruger at the general store. Kruger was old now and welcomed the help. John slept on a cot bed in the back of the store, and for a man brought up to better things he never complained. But then,

Josh reasoned, the man was a soldier and hardship came naturally.

Often they would sit and talk, usually on two old battered rocking-chairs that Josh had placed just outside his office. It gave a good view down the main street and a fine look at the sunset. Josh would talk about his past; the army, never settling, never marrying, and about the war. He spoke disparagingly of his career as a lawman. John disagreed; in his opinion Josh had a fine sense of duty and care for the town he defended.

'Josh,' he said one evening, 'I have searched Arabella high and low for a fully-fledged sheriff for you to be deputy to but I have to confess that I have come up empty handed. Is it not perhaps the right moment for a promotion?'

'Deputies get paid a lot less than sheriffs, son. I guess the Governor is just a careful man.'

John talked usually of England, of his family and sometimes of Marianne, the girl back in Canada whose beauty had inadvertently caused a man to die and John to become a fugitive.

At other times, John Carshalton helped the preacher's wife, Mrs Harrison, to teach the few children that Arabella boasted, to read and write. Arabella as yet had no school or church, but a room at the back of the saloon was made available for both.

The school operated in the mornings when the saloon was closed and the saloon girls kept themselves well out of sight. On Sunday morning, they joined the more respectable of Arabella's citizenship to pray and sing hymns. Whores and settlers, wives, gamblers and farmers shared a prayer book and a good thought in a spirit of tolerance that would last just about as long as it took for the town to become what is generally called 'civilized'.

John had become one with this strange world. He was well liked by most menfolk, who sensed the soldier in him, the quiet strength, and the hint of danger. The women mainly loved him. The older women adored his precise British accent and his impeccable manners when near ladies, the younger women fluttered about him, hoping to catch his eye. Both the saloon girls in particular loved him for one thing: he treated all women as ladies.

One in particular, Connie Brady, thought John one of the most handsome men she had ever met and was often his companion for a drink at the Drover's Rest.

Concepta Brady was from a good Irish Catholic family but had become pregnant by a handsome cousin from Donegal. She had fled in her shame to give birth in a convent in Chicago. Her child was taken from her to be fostered she knew not where, and she then endured the cruelty of the nuns until she could take no more and stole enough money to get a train West.

Like the other girl, she would have gladly provided John with a night's comfort at no charge, but with both of them he pretended not to understand.

Instead he and Connie became close friends and often after the saloon had closed and Connie, as was usual, had no customers, she would come to the little room at the back of the store, where they would share a pot of tea and he would read to her.

Connie had never learned to read despite the brief and concentrated attentions of the Sisters of Mercy, and John would read to her each night from The Pickwick Papers by Mr Charles Dickens.

Connie would sit wrapped in a crocheted shawl that had been her mother's, sipping tea and listening to the adventures of a pompous and kindly old gentleman and his assortment of well-meaning friends as they travelled through the lanes and villages of a country that now lay on the other side of the world.

She would frown with worry and concern as the Pickwickians got into scrape after scrape, and clap her hands and squeal with laughter at the ridiculousness of it all. In those moments, when the years of hardship momentarily fell away, she looked the age she was, just twenty, with the beautiful black hair and dark eyes of an Irish beauty.

John offered to teach her to read, but that would have defeated the object for Connie, which was to spend time with John, and to listen to the stories being read in that gentle English accent, that while not always welcome in her native Ireland, still reminded her of home.

The evenings always finished with John giving her a squeeze of the hand and a light kiss on the cheek as she stepped out into the night.

Some men wondered out loud if his tastes actually ran the other way. Josh knew different. He knew that John had only one woman in his life and she was far north of the Canadian border.

Then one morning, when the stagecoach made its regular stop, there was a letter for J. Carshalton, Esq., Care of Arabella, Kansas.

John sat in his room at the back of the store and read:

My dearest John,

Words cannot say how much I am missing you and how much the few messages you have been able to send to me have meant. My heart is full that you are at last a little settled and it seems that you are among friends.

The great hue and cry after the duel has now subsided but as you would expect, you are posted as a deserter and would face a court martial on your return.

The thing that rests so heavy on my heart is that you did what you did for me, to support my desire to resist the unwanted suit that was being pressed upon me by Monsieur Cottin. I am beyond grief that I have been the cause of so much hardship for you, of so much unjust and unwarranted slander.

Which brings me to the thing of which I must tell you, must warn you. Cottin's brother Andre has vowed his vengeance. He has vowed to find you and challenge you on the field of honour. Oh, but dearest John, I do not trust him. Captain Charles Cadbury, who has been as dear and loyal a friend to me as he always has been to you, has had the distasteful little man checked up upon. We know that he has travelled by ship to New Orleans, and there he has hired the services of a professional assassin known as De Saille. Our informant believes that these men know of your whereabouts and are travelling to you.

John, please do not bring more trouble upon your head on account of me.

Please avoid the trouble that is following you. I fear for your safety and I fear for you becoming involved in something that might make you an outlaw in America. I know how strongly you feel about matters of honour and I know you will face this man if he challenges you

Please my darling, whilst my heart aches to see you again, it will mean so much just to know that you are safe.

Leave now, my darling, and contact me again only when it is safe to do so. Know that you are always in my thoughts and my prayers and my heart.

Your true love

Marianne

John Carshalton, son of Sir Humphrey Carshalton, and a captain in the 60th Royal Rifles, sat in the back room of a small general store in a dusty little Kansas town thousands of miles from his home and cried silently and for a very long time.

That afternoon, sitting on the porch outside the jailhouse sharing a bottle of rough rye whiskey, Josh felt his friend's sadness. He waited in the hope that information would be volunteered but when it was not forthcoming he was forced to ask.

'Something troubling you, boy?'

John opened his mouth for denial, then looked into the eyes of the older man. His shoulders sagged and he nodded. He took the letter from his pocket and passed it to Josh, who took a battered pair of spectacles from his vest pocket and placed them on his nose. He read slowly, his lips moving over the words, sometimes having to go back, his eyes screwing slightly with concentration. When at last he finished he handed the letter back and looked thoughtfully at the sky, puffing gently on the clay pipe.

'So what do you figure to do?'

'I have no choice.'

'Hell boy, you always have a choice.'

'Marianne is right. I must move on.'

'Now hold on there just a minute, son. With the greatest of respect to the young lady, I suggest she is not in possession of all the facts.'

'On the contrary, Josh, she seems to be in possession of a great deal more facts than I. For I knew nothing of the actions of Monsieur Cottin.'

'I'll give you that, but it ain't what I meant. I meant she ain't in possession of the facts concerning your place here.'

'My place?'

'Yes, God dammit, your place. Boy, you've fitted in here better than a rainstorm in a dry spell. Folks here got time for you, like you, respect you.'

'And I like them. All the more reason I should move on and not attract a fanatic like Cottin and some professional assassin.'

'And where do you run to?'

'I have not yet given that much thought.'

'Damn right, you haven't. 'Cause wherever it is, sure as hell it will be somewhere. And somewhere has folks just like these ones. John, you can't run from people like this. I know you ain't afraid, not in that way, I've never seen a man with a harder edge to him when the going gets tough, but what I mean is that trouble will find you one way or another. It might as well be here as any place else.'

John had scarcely ever heard Josh talk so long or so passionately. He sighed, his head was in turmoil.

'There is much in what you say, my friend, but the man Cottin brings with him is a professional, and we do not know if they bring others. We are . . .' he struggled for the right words. 'We are not best placed for such a confrontation.'

'Meaning, "just one old timer with a slow gun hand", huh?'

'No, no, that is not what I meant at all.'

'You did, son, and it's true. But that ain't the end of it. I still have friends, and I'm still owed some favours. If I can tell you that I can bring a lawman down here who will not only stand with us but just as like as not there won't even be a shot fired. What would you say then?'

John looked sadly out at Arabella's main street, slow and lazy in the afternoon.

'I would say, Josh, that I will stay. But I am afraid, afraid that I am going to bring a lot of trouble to people that I like.'

And so it was, a week later that Marshal Jess Coleman found himself sitting in the office of Mayor Edwin Bird Allen, the first mayor of Wichita.

'Jess, all I'm asking is for you to ride down there and keep an eye on things.' Allen leaned back in the padded chair and stroked the long pointed beard trimmed as neatly as his long dark hair. He gazed at the ceiling for a moment then lowered his eyes again to look directly at Marshal Coleman, who was sitting as he always did, back to the wall, chair tilted at an angle that defied gravity, staring at his hat as it turned slowly in his hand.

'Don't know, Mr Mayor, there's another drive coming in early next week. We're going to be busy as hell.'

'Hell, the drives are no trouble any more, Jess, you know that. Just noise, nothing more.'

'Look, Joshua is a good man and I know you two go back a long way, but he runs a slack town. He lets too many saddle bums keep their guns. Hell, he even lets the town drunk keep his gun. It's just been dumb luck he's never had a killing. Now he's buying himself a mess of trouble. Why? All he has to do is move the Englishman on. The trouble will move with him.'

'The man helped him out of a spot. He figures he owes him.'

'A spot he would never have been in if he made men leave their guns. Damn it, Ed. It's been waiting to happen.'

Allen smiled serenely and gazed upward again. He had ridden Jess's storms before; they soon blew out.

'So, you can go down there and tell him you told him so.'

'Dammed if I won't!'

'And while you're there you can stop anybody getting killed.'

Jess scowled at the mayor whilst the significance of this sank in. Then he could not prevent a soft laugh.

'Damn you, Ed, you always get your way with me.'

'That's why they made me mayor, son, because I'm persuasive.'

'Two Frenchmen, you say?'

'That's what I'm told. I'm waiting for a wire from New Orleans but Josh thinks only one of them is a gunfighter.'

'Josh wouldn't know a gunfighter from a horse's ass. All right, I'll get over there, but just as soon as you have something on these two, I want to hear it.'

FIVE

'Josh, what damn fool mess have you got yourself into this time?'

'Good to see you too, Jess.'

Josh finished pouring the coffee, handed a cup to Jess and slumped back into his seat. The marshal was sitting on the corner of a table looking out of the window down the small main street of Arabella.

'Well, damn it, man! You are a lawman; your job is to keep the peace. Not go looking for trouble.'

'Well, I didn't exactly go looking for trouble, Jess. I had a problem to sort and the Englishman helped me out. I owe him.'

'And if you got strangers to leave their guns here when they arrived, you would not have had a problem.'

'Fine for you to say. I don't have twenty deputies

to cover every way into town. I have me, and I have to sleep. I watch what I can and I make it my business to get to know every stranger I see. It may not be perfect but it will just have to do.'

Jess shrugged, conceding the point.

'True enough. But the fact remains that you should send the Englishman packing. Keep the trouble moving.'

'You, sir, have taken the very words from my mouth.'

They both turned to see John standing in the doorway. Jess rose to his feet feeling uncharacteristically awkward.

Josh spread his hand at Jess. 'Jess Coleman, meet Captain John Carshalton of the British army.'

For a moment Jess expected an unpleasant reaction from the young man but instead he moved forward and offered his hand to Jess. He bowed instinctively; 'Your servant.'

Josh smiled and informed Jess dryly, 'He promises that to everyone but I saw him first.'

John ignored the jibe.

'I take you to be the marshal that Josh spoke of?'

Jess accepted the outstretched hand. The grip was firm and he noted with grudging approval that the Englishman looked him steadily in the eye.

'That's me, Captain Carshalton. I guess you weren't meant to hear that last speech.'

'You have said nothing I have not already said to Josh. I took a great deal of persuading to stay. If it is your considered opinion that it would be the best course of action for me to leave, I will do so without hesitation.'

Jess looked relieved.

'Well, sir, I guess I only said what I planned to say to your face.'

'Now hold on just a damn minute,' Josh was on his feet. 'We have been through this, and we have agreed. Running from here will solve nothing.' He turned on Jess. 'Is that how we are going to deal with trouble, Jess? A couple of Frenchies come up from New Orleans and we send an innocent man packing? An' afore you say nothing Jess, John has committed no crime in the United States, and for that matter what he did in Canada was to kill a man in a fair fight. If we don't protect people what the hell kind of law, are we? Word will get back from here to the Mississippi; if you want to hunt someone down, do it in Kansas, their law run scared.'

Jess could not quite hide a smile. It was an out-burst he himself would have been proud of. He held up a hand to calm Josh down.

'Now just hold on, old man. Nobody said any-thing about running away. Now that you put me in the mind, maybe all we are doing is pushing the problem on to someone else.'

He turned to John. 'Tell me about the men who are coming.'

'I only know one; Andre Cottin, a vicious little scoundrel but nevertheless not a man who would become involved in what he would consider common brawling. He comes only to kill me. He will have no desire to engage in any sort of conflict with either Josh or yourself. That is why he brings the other man, who we know only by reputation as a hired killer.'

Josh nodded. 'All I could get is that he is not wanted for anything in any of the states of the union. He seems to have managed to make a lot of money from killing without ever having anything pinned on him.'

'So he's smart,' Jess nodded thoughtfully. 'So much the better. If he's smart he will see what the odds are and hand over his gun. We will put them both on the next train out of Abilene and tell them that we ever see their murdering hides in Kansas again they will spend the rest of their lives here.'

'So no one will get hurt?' John still looked uncertain.

Jess smiled and winked. 'That's why I'm here, son.'

SIX

The late summer sun was beating down on De Saille and Cottin as they rode North West to Arabella.

De Saille had sensibly changed into loose fitting pants and an open-necked blouse. He wore a wide brimmed hat against the sun. He had however kept his high shiny boots into which the pants were tucked.

Cottin, on the other hand, still wore the suit in which he had travelled, and ordinary shoes. The suit was crumpled and covered with the fine dust of the trail. On his head he wore a white military sun helmet. He looked and felt ridiculous.

The flies had been swarming around them all day, and the brush that they passed seemed to crackle in the heat as though about to ignite at any moment. De Saille rode slightly in front, the better to shut his ears to the incessant complaining of his companion. He now wanted only to get the job done, and for this foolish little man to exact his equally foolish and misplaced revenge.

He tried instead to concentrate on the countryside around him. Harsh and wild it was, but undeniably impressive. He had fallen in love with this vast continent the first time he set foot in Canada. He had been angry about his expulsion by the British, whom he thought hypocrites who travelled the world beating other nations into submission with some of the most sadistic and cutthroat men ever to put on an army uniform, who then become righteously indignant over a man who was paid to kill.

He came to America partly from necessity, as he could never return to France nor did he have any desire to. However, he found that the newness of this still untamed country appealed to him. A harsh voice cut across his thoughts.

'Stay nice and still there, mister. I think you and I need to discuss things.'

He swung around in the saddle and there on an outcrop of rocks was Kyle, crouching slightly, a rifle aimed at De Saille's chest.

De Saille relaxed slightly and looked Kyle in the

eye. 'Is this how you show gratitude for saving your life?'

Kyle lowered the rifle. 'Oh don't get me wrong, mister. I'm sure grateful enough. It's just that when a man does something like that for a stranger, I have to get to wondering why.'

De Saille simply shrugged.

Kyle considered this for a moment then laughed softly.

'Well, dammit, sir, that is good enough for me. Now see here, what sort of man would I be if I didn't offer you some fresh-brewed coffee, and some good biscuits? Will you join us, sir?'

De Saille turned to Cottin who had understood little of the exchange but recognized Kyle from the day before.

'We are taking a rest, my friend.'

'Is that wise?'

'Coffee is always wise when you are thirsty, and I am thirsty.'

'These are the men who robbed that bank.'

'I am well aware of that.'

'Then they are thieves.'

'If they planned to do any harm, they would have done it by now. I for one welcome the rest. Come.'

They rode for about a mile, Kyle and De Saille

riding side by side and Cottin sulkily bringing up the rear. Close to another crop of boulders, they came upon Wills and Jones sprawled around a small campfire.

At their approach, Wills was on his feet with his gun drawn, He relaxed slightly when he saw Kyle, but scowled at De Saille and Cortin.

'Damn it, Kyle. I wasn't expecting three riders. I darn nearly blew your head off.'

'Take it easy, Wills. That jumpy way of yours is going to get somebody hurt.'

He swept his hand at the two Frenchmen. 'These here are my two good friends, Monsieur Noel De Saille and Monsieur Andre Cottin.' He pronounced it 'mon sewer' whether deliberately or not, De Saille could not be sure. 'All the way from Paris, France.'

De Saille thought of mentioning that neither of them had ever been to Paris but decided it was not worth it.

'And why in hell are you bringing them here?'

'Because Monsieur De Saille is the one who slipped me a gun yesterday when that old fool had a bead on me. I guess I owe him a cup of coffee.'

Wills shook his head. 'I cannot figure you, Kyle, Lord knows I try but I cannot figure you.'

'Well then, best you leave the figuring to me,

young Wills, and you get to fixing some coffee.'

Jones did not join in this exchange. Instead he sat looking morosely at the horizon. He had ridden with Penny for a number of years. He was feeling the loss bitterly.

They made themselves comfortable around the fire; Cottin, still silent and aloof, sat well away from the circle, but took a mug of coffee when it was offered.

'I do have to say this, De Saille,' Kyle said once he was comfortably sprawled against his saddle, 'you are a cool one. When everybody else scattered you sat there, cool as you please.'

'I was enjoying the show.'

'Were you, now?'

'It was very well planned. It deserved to succeed.'

'So it did, so it did. It would have if that mad old coot hadn't started blasting away. What riles me is two saddle-bags full of good Yankee dollars left in the middle of the street.'

Jones spoke for the first time. 'What riles me, Kyle, is a good friend left in the middle of the street.'

'He knew the risks same as all of us, Jones. I didn't notice you so cut up you wanted to stay around when I told you to git.'

74

'You saying I was yeller?'

'I'm saying you used your head, so keep using it. Penny's dead and gone. It was bad luck was all.' He turned to De Saille, 'What was happening when you left?'

'A great deal of excitement, as you might imagine. There was talk of getting together a group of men to come after you.'

'I figured there would be a posse. We've outrun posses before. Mostly store clerks and stable hands who think they're shootists. I ain't too bothered. So where are you two headed?'

'A little town to the west of here, over the border in Kansas, Arabella.'

'The hell you say! We were there ourselves a few months back. Had a little bit of trouble. So why have you come all this way to finish up there?'

'To kill a man?'

'Well now, I guess I did figure you right. You're a hired gun?'

'That confuses me with the kind of thugs that cattle men hire to frighten sheep farmers. I am a professional assassin.'

'Are you now? And just who is it that you are off to professionally assassinate, if I might be so bold as to ask?'

'Not I, on this occasion. I am merely here to support my companion. It is he who will do the killing.'

Kyle looked over De Saille's shoulder at Cottin, and guffawed loudly. 'Him? That little popinjay is going to kill a man?'

'Oh yes. On the field of honour, of course. He is going to fight a duel.'

'A duel?'

'You are familiar with the term, I trust.'

'Yeah, guy told me about it once. Said it still goes on in Europe. Something about standing there in the wide open while somebody counts to ten and then you shoot at each other. The most damn fool way of fighting I ever heard tell.'

'I am very inclined to agree with you, but none the less that is what he is going to do.'

'And there's some other damn fool, prepared to meet him?'

'There is . . . an Englishman.'

'Say what?'

'An Englishman named Carshalton.'

'Well, I will be damned.' Kyle thought for a moment and came to his decision. 'Yes, sir, I will be damned.'

De Saille watched the other man curiously. 'You

seem to have the advantage over me, *monsieur*.'

'When I said we had some trouble, that interfering Englishman was at the back of it.'

'Was he, now?'

'He was, and we had every intention to go back and settle with him, except. . . .'

'Except?'

'Except I have heard that him and that ol' timer deputy got some help.'

'Really?'

'Marshal Jess Coleman.'

'I do not know the name.'

'You would if you rode these parts. He's the worst kind of lawman; he's fast, he's hard and he cannot be bought.'

De Saille leaned back against a rock and frowned. It was perhaps what he had feared. It made things more difficult, if not impossible. The main concern was that the only explanation for the arrival of this lawman was that Carshalton had been warned of their intentions. The element of surprise had gone.

He drained the last of his coffee and looked across at Cottin, who was now surrendering to weariness and was leaning back with his eyes closed.

The venture had been possible when all he had to do was hold one man back while Cottin enacted

77

his foolish ritual. Now with a marshal present there was no way the duel could go ahead uninterrupted. He would be forced into killing two lawmen probably in front of witnesses. He could become a man with a price on his head. The rules had changed.

The logical approach was to turn round and head back to New Orleans. Kyle was watching carefully.

'Not what you wanted to hear, I guess?'

'You guess correctly.'

'Strikes me we might be able to transact some business here.'

'I do not understand.'

'We had business in Arabella three months ago when Wills got himself in a fight with the town drunk and that Englishmen interfered when I had the drop on the deputy.'

'From what I have heard of Arabella, I cannot imagine there would be much worth robbing.'

'And there you would be wrong.'

De Saille waited.

'Seventy-five thousand dollars on their way to Fort Scott.'

'You are going to take on the army?'

'Nope. Just one old stagecoach driver.'

Kyle saw the look of disbelief on the Frenchman's

face. 'Oh it's guarded. Two men riding shotgun. I have a contact at the bank at Abilene where they fill the box. Army sees it filled and locked then it goes on the stage like it was a box full of women's corsets.'

'So why in Arabella – why not out on the open road?'

'Fair question – that's the clever bit. Arabella is where the eastbound and the westbound stages cross over.'

De Saille frowned; it was beginning to make sense.

'The eastbound – the one with the money – waits in Arabella until a company of soldiers turn up late morning to escort it on to Fort Scott. The shotgun guards change on to the westbound stage and head back. For four hours that stage sits in Arabella being guarded by our old buddy the deputy sheriff. We go in, take it and retire from the business.'

De Saille frowned. 'You trust your contact?'

'Well enough.'

De Saille looked unconvinced but simply shrugged; it was not of great moment to him.

'Now I was a mite concerned about Jess Coleman showing up,' Kyle continued, 'but now I know why it could work out well.'

De Saille looked amused. 'I am sure you will tell me how.'

'Well now, my boys, and don't get me wrong, they are stout fellows right enough but not the best gunmen I have ever seen. Now, if you are good enough with a gun to make a living at it, and I ain't no slouch myself, I think we might be able to come to a business agreement.'

'I am listening.'

'I can see that you are. Good, because I think we can make this work so that we all get what we want.'

Later, de Saille outlined the plan to Cortin in a hushed conversation in French, Cortin voiced his objections.

'Are you insane? These men are barbarians.'

'I am joining them for their guns, not for their table manners.'

'We are not joining them at all. This is not what we agreed. I have a reputation to consider. I cannot be dragged into some sordid robbery.'

'And taking on a US marshal is not what we agreed. You need have nothing to do with the robbery. They will commit their crime and you will conduct your "business" without interruption. Frankly, Cottin, it is this way or we turn and ride back, because no US marshal is going to stand around whilst you conduct a duel, however gentle-manly it is, in the middle of his territory.'

Cottin shook his head wearily. 'I do so hate this awful country.'

SEVEN

It had been Kyle's considered opinion that the posse from Tremaine would almost certainly head south. 'They will be chasing their tails for days,' he predicted, 'unless they get lucky.'

So it was the nature of the way things were going for Kyle and his companions that the posse got lucky.

The two Frenchmen and the three Americans were just a day's ride out from Arabella when the posse, who were just deciding to cut through to Abilene, spotted them from a ridge. They would indeed have had the element of surprise had not one of posse believed his hunting rifle capable of a greater range than it actually possessed. The shot was enough to get the heads of the five men jerking around to see the dozen or so horses on the skyline.

Without a word, the three outlaws spurred their horses into a gallop, followed quickly by De Saille and a cursing Cottin. They headed for another ridge about a mile away as the posse swarmed down each side of their rocky slope and took off in pursuit across the open plain.

Just when Kyle had decided that his luck could get no worse, it arranged to do precisely that. They rode into a small couloir between two high boulders of rock, both with sheer faces, that looked to all the world as though it led through to the open prairie beyond. It did not. It terminated instead in yet another sheer rock face. They had ridden into a dead end. They were trapped.

'Get down and take cover.'

Kyle realized what an unnecessary order this was as the riders were already off their horses and scrambling for what cover there was amongst the small outcrops of rocks, barking knees and shins in their haste to find some kind of safety.

'Let 'em come!' Kyle shouted. 'We'll have them like fish in a barrel.'

Sheriff Coogan, meanwhile, was having trouble keeping his group of volunteers alive; in some cases he was wondering why he was bothering.

It seemed impossible that the order and usual

calm of his life could have been shattered so suddenly. Since the robbery his life had been a misery.

It had begun there in the main street of Tremaine, where Coogan had stood, still feeling sick and in pain, as Mayor Bentley had borne down upon him. Bentley saw every event in one of two ways: this is politically good for Bentley, or this is politically bad for Bentley. It did not take a political genius to predict which one of these Bentley believed applied to the situation as the smoke from the robbed bank drifted gently over two corpses in Main Street, one of them a respected citizen of Tremaine.

'Well, Coogan,' Bentley snapped, 'and what do you intend to do about all this?'

Coogan suspected that what he intended to do immediately was to be violently sick over Bentley's brightly polished shoes, but instead he fought down another wave of nausea and tried to clear his head.

'Let me help you here, Sheriff Coogan.' Bentley took Coogan's silence as indecision. 'You will raise a posse and take off after that scum and do it while the trail is still fresh.'

'Frankly, Mr Bentley, what I would sooner do is take a deputy and start to track them myself. I'm no lover of posses.'

84

'And I'm no lover of having my town shot up and its citizens killed. You can see the mood these people are in.'

'I can see exactly what mood these people are in and that is why I do not want hot-headed trigger-happy amateurs going up against hardened gunmen. There have been enough people hurt.'

Some of the crowd were overhearing the increasingly loud disagreement and a general grumbling was growing. Coogan's war record with the US army did not play well with many of the citizens of Tremaine. Whilst they conceded he was a good lawman, having a dammed Yankee with a badge was not to everybody's taste. Bentley caught the mood and acted with a politician's instinct.

'These good people have a right to protect their town, Coogan, especially when those paid to do so have failed. I order you to raise a posse now and hunt these men.'

So it was, then, that Coogan found himself trying to hold back men foolish enough to ride straight towards armed men who, although having ridden into a dead end, still had the advantage, for the small canyon narrowed until scarcely three horsemen abreast could ride through. The outlaws would be able to concentrate fire on that narrow space and cause mayhem.

'Hold back, boys, for the love of God!'

They reined in, just out of range of the rifles of the men crouched amongst the rocks, the horses milling about, kicking up the dust as men grumbled and swore.

Amongst the rocks, no small amount of grumbling and swearing was also taking place. Cottin, in particular, was beside himself with rage. He launched a stream of abuse at De Saille, cursing him for involving them with desperadoes, for putting them on the wrong side of the law and jeopardizing his chance to exact revenge on John Carshalton.

As the abuse was in French, it was unintelligible to the three outlaws but was still expressive enough to strongly suggest its nature. Kyle thought seriously for a moment of shooting the Frenchman to silence him, but he knew he needed De Saille and this was no time for fighting amongst themselves.

He had seen the sheriff regain control of the posse, and knew that any hope he had of a reckless charge that would have allowed them to reduce the numbers had gone. He was going to have to think their way out of this and he suspected that De Saille had brain as well as a gun hand to offer.

EIGHT

At the time that Kyle and the others were riding out, headed towards their unplanned rendezvous with the posse, John was receiving a letter from the early morning stage. He knew at once that it came from Marianne. He took it away to the back of the store and sat down to read.

My dearest John,
Please forgive me as I have not written to you in such a while but so much has happened to me over the last few weeks that I do not know where to begin.

Under the strain of the last few months Captain Cadbury has been a rock, and a loyal and true friend.

So much time have we spent together that a bond has formed between us and this has grown over the days and weeks. It was not something that either of us planned, my dearest, but we have grown closer and discover that we have a great and true affection for one another.

In short we have fallen in love and decided that the only course that can make us happy is to be wed, which we intend to do once the banns have been read.

I know this will come as a shock to you, John, and it was never the intention of either of us to hurt you. We neither of us suspected that this would be the outcome of our association. It is an outcome that we could not control.

I know this news may upset you and I pray with all my soul that in the fullness of time you may find it in your heart to forgive. Please do not be angry with your friend Charles, I cannot describe his distress at the hurt that he may be causing you.

I know in my heart that you too will find the happiness that Charles and I now share.

I wish you only peace and contentment, and most of all I wish you to be safe and well.

Please take the very best care of yourself and know that you will always be in my heart and my prayers.

Your special friend,

Marianne

This time John did not cry. He did not at that moment feel like crying. Indeed he felt little at all.

He went to the stables, saddled his Pilot and rode out of town on to the prairie. He rode out of the stables at full gallop, causing many heads to turn including that of Connie, who was hanging out sheets from the upper windows of the saloon.

As he rode John's anger grew, an intense, painful anger of the kind he had never felt before, the pain of betrayal, of hurt pride, of intense loneliness.

He drove the horse into a gallop, digging his heels harder and harder into its flanks. This was a cavalry horse that knew how to run and John had it at a full charge, the dust flying up around them. He drove the horse spitefully and meanly, not releasing it from the full charge but driving it harder still. He could feel the pain of the animal, see its eyes beginning to start from their sockets. He was screaming at the terrified animal to ride faster and faster.

And then it was gone. A stab of guilt went

through him; he reined the horse to a stop and jumped down. Pilot was panting, swaying slightly, his body covered in sweat and there were flecks of foam around his mouth.

John spoke softly, gently stroking his mane. After a while, Pilot began to calm and John turned him and began to lead him back, still not prepared to mount. After a mile or so they came on a small stream, but he held the horse back, ensured that he had cooled sufficiently and collected water in his hat. He wet his hand and ran it across Pilot's muzzle. Finally he allowed the animal to drink slowly, but he was calmer now and after a while began to nuzzle against him. At last John remounted and began to ride slowly back towards Arabella.

As he rode he realized that for the first time since leaving Canada he felt oppressively lonely. He thought about Northumberland, about his home and his parents. About riding through Kielder forest on a clear frosty morning, to return to a log fire and the fruit scones that the cook knew were his favourites.

He tried to fathom what he was doing in this strange, wild country. Why he had let himself be persuaded to run from the only job he had ever wanted to do by a man who was only furthering his own ends and his own desires. He felt wretchedly foolish. He thought of the last words of Marianne's letter: your special friend. Of all the awful words in that awful letter those three words hurt him the most.

Back in Arabella, Connie had seen him ride out. She had seen the look on his face and the way he smacked his horse into a reckless gallop. She had seen anger in him that she had never seen before in this quietly spoken Englishman.

She went at once to the little back room of the store. She had no hesitation in going in. This was their special place, a place where she had found that a man could want her company for something other than her body. A place where she had rested back against the single pillow on the small cot bed and let John transport her to the silly, comic, wonderful world of the pompous, gentle, well-meaning Mr Pickwick.

The letter lay on the small bed. She picked it up and even though she could not read she could not resist letting her eyes run over it as though she could, over the small neat handwriting. She lifted it to her nose to smelt the faint perfume still there even after many days in mail sacks on many stagecoaches and trains.

She crossed the street into Josh's office. He was busy stripping down the arsenal that he held in his office, which consisted of three breech loading Springfield rifles and four pistols. They lay in bits on the oilcloth as Josh carefully and skilfully assured himself that every working part would function. It was army training that had kept him alive then and he believed it would do so again.

Connie held out the letter to him. 'Read it to me.'

'What is it?'

'It's John's. It is from that woman in Canada.'

'Then it's private.'

'I do not give a damn. John just rode out here as though half the Indian nations were after him. I want to know why.'

Josh still hesitated. Connie leaned forward into Josh's face.

'We are his friends. If he is in trouble we need to know.'

Josh snorted. 'One thing we can always be sure of with that young man is that he is always in trouble.'

'Just read it.'

Josh sighed and picked up his battered spectacles. He read the letter out loud, slowly, stumbling over some of the words. As Connie listened her face darkened with anger.

'The bitch!' she said simply when he had finished. 'The selfish little French bitch.' She turned to leave. 'I'm going after him.'

'You know where he's gone?'

'No.'

'Connie, you cannot ride worth a damn, and even if you could you have no idea where he is. He will be back.'

'She's hurt him, Josh.'

'That she has, but it's a hurt a lot of people have. He is a lot tougher than you think.'

'I would like to kill her,' Connie said with a chilling simplicity.

'I am sure you would but, as you do not have the means to get to Canada she will probably survive.'

Lost for any other empty threats to utter, Connie turned and stormed out of the office.

While John was riding slowly back to town, a hundred miles away five men who all, for various reasons, wanted him dead were crouched amongst the rocks at the bottom of a sheer rock face on the Kansas-Missouri border.

At the moment it was a stand-off. The odd shot

was being fired from either side to keep heads down but other than that they sat miserably in the late afternoon sunshine. Kyle knew that the initiative lay with the sheriff and his posse. They could afford to wait, or go for reinforcements. One way or the other the outlaws were going to have to break out of this.

Wills had been thoughtfully studying the rock face. 'I can climb it.'

Kyle turned to follow his gaze. 'The hell you can.'

'Can so.'

'OK, so you can climb it. You will be picked off before you are a quarter of the way up.'

'I will wait until dark.'

'You will climb that in the dark?'

'Easy.'

'OK. You climb without being spotted and without breaking your fool neck. You get all the way to the top.'

'That's the idea.'

'So what,' Kyle asked wearily, 'do you do then? Go for help?'

Wills scowled. It was true that he had not thought any further than climbing the rock face. He mumbled something about getting round behind the posse but Kyle had already lost interest and had returned to gloomily trying to figure out an escape route. Wills sat sulkily back against a rock and lapsed into silence.

Kyle turned to De Saille. 'We'll wait until dark and ride straight through them. They're mostly amateurs. With a bit of luck they won't be able to hit a thing.'

De Saille was never one to trust to luck. 'I agree we wait until dark. However I think I can lessen the odds of anyone getting hurt.'

The late evening sun was fading in the west when John rode slowly back into town. He took his horse back to the livery stable where young Charlie Rhodes, the blacksmith's son, took him. He looked enquiringly at John but said nothing.

When John emerged from the stable he saw Josh sitting on the porch with a jug beside him. John crossed the street and joined Josh on the porch. Without a word he sank wearily into the chair beside the deputy sheriff. Josh passed him the jug and he took a long pull, longer than was his custom, before handing it back.

They sat in silence for a while, and then at last Josh took the crumpled letter from his pocket and handed it to John.

'Connie took it. I told her it was wrong, that it was private, but you know what women are like when they get riled.'

'Connie was upset?'

'Hell boy, she was fit to ride to Canada and do her some killing.'

'You read it to her?'

'With Connie coming at me with eyes blazing like coals of hell, you bet your ass I read it to her.'

There was more silence while John digested this along with some more contents of the jug.

'Well, you were right.'

'I was?'

'The first night we met you told me I had behaved like a horse's arse. Well that is certainly what I feel like at this moment.'

'Never as easy as that, John. It's tough for women.'

'I beg your pardon?'

'I say it's tough for women. Don't matter none how high born they are or how rich their folks is. They have to rely on a man to look out for them, to get them the things they want, things they need. You weren't there. By all accounts she's a looker. No surprise that somebody else stepped in.'

'I did not think it would be my best friend.'

'A good-looking woman has a habit of putting a bit of strain on friendships.'

'So it would seem,' John sighed wearily. 'Josh, for the first time in my life, I have no idea what to do next.'

'I'll tell you what to do next. Go back to your crib. I have work to do and you need the rest.'

When Josh had risen and gone back inside the office John was left a little surprised and hurt by his friend's abrupt manner. He sat for a while watching the sky darken and the starts brighten, then he rose and crossed the street to the general store.

When he entered the back room it was in darkness and he had to fumble with the lamp to get it lit. As the room brightened he became aware that he was not alone. Connie rose slightly out of the narrow bed in the corner. He could see enough of her to know that she was naked. She pulled the sheet aside slightly to reinforce that understanding. He had always known that she was pretty, now he realized how pretty, as she pulled the covers away from a body, ivory white against her dark hair, pleasingly soft and rounded. For all that her life had been up until now, lying there on the small cot in the small bare store room, she looked innocent, and vulnerable and lovely.

He stood staring at her, uncertain. Connie spoke quietly but firmly.

'Don't say a thing. Just get those clothes off and get in here with me. I'm going to make you feel better.'

When he slipped in beside her, and felt the smoothness of her skin and let his hands explore her soft body, causing little whimpers, he knew it felt right.

After a short while he was able to concede that she was indeed making him feel very much better.

NINE

Noel De Saille was born in Marseilles in 1831, the third child of a whore who succumbed to the pox four years later, leaving De Saille just one of many street urchins struggling to survive.

With the various French conquests in the early part of the century Marseilles had grown into a thriving port and industrial centre.

With prosperity came opportunity for all, including the ragged children running wild in the streets. By the time he was nine De Saille was already a successful pimp, managing girls only a few years older than he. He hated the work but it brought food and shelter and he was good at it.

When he was eleven a sailor, badly underestimating the skinny child, cheerfully refused to pay for the whore he had just used. De Saille simply broke a bottle and attacked with such ferocity that the man was already bleeding to death before he had time to defend himself. De Saille sat and watched him die with deep interest and was puzzled by the feeling of accomplishment and deep satisfaction that it gave him.

So enjoyable had been the sensation that he found himself offering to dispose of the enemy of one of his street acquaintances. Not only did this prove every bit as satisfactory but the acquaintance also paid him for his trouble. Almost overnight De Saille had found himself a new line of work, which earned him a comfortable living as the years went on.

The new thriving Marseilles did not want the dubious distinction of having one of the country's youngest mass murders on its streets. De Saille was caught, tried and sentenced to death. However, deciding that an execution of one so young would also fail to serve in the best interests of the citizens, the sentence was commuted and the judges decided there was better use to be put to his extraordinary talents. De Saille was persuaded to volunteer for the French Foreign Legion of the basis that he had been born in one of the French colonies, and having been an outcast and outside the law all his life, nobody could dispute it, and few cared to bother.

Officially at least, no Frenchmen served in the legion which was full of disparate, desperate, hard-cases from all over Europe. De Saille liked the company but hated the discipline.

De Saille's army career lasted three short years but during that he time, although he saw little real action, he learned new skills and earned a reputation as a man cool under fire and merciless in a fight. He was feared and respected at once by both officers and men.

That is, with one notable exception; Sergeant Chef Rudi Meir, a former German mercenary and as unpleasant a man as ever rose to NCO in the Legion. Hated and feared by most of the men. He was simply hated by De Saille.

In 1863, De Saille was amongst the first two battalions of Legionnaires sent to invade Mexico to persuade it to honour foreign debts. The reason for the invasion bothered De Saille little but, he hoped, would give him a golden opportunity to do some real fighting. It was not to be. Early in the campaign under the leadership of a weak and sickly sous-lieutenant they marched in search of an enemy that knew the land a great deal better than they did. And when the officer died Rudi Meir took charge and the ill-fated operation went from bad to worse. Late one afternoon, when exhausted men lay trying to recover from another long forced march, Meir walked around cursing the men for their laziness and cowardice.

He made the mistake – inevitably fatal – of kicking De Saille. De Saille rose without complaint, took his bayonet from its scabbard, examined it carefully, then calmly and without any great urgency, stabbed the bully several times. Then he sat beside him as he died, explaining quite where it was that he had made serious errors of judgement.

When the man was dead De Saille shook hands with his companions, wished them a safe return and started off North towards the United States of America.

Apart from a brief business venture in Canada, which had resulted in the British running him back south of the border, America was where De Saille had settled.

It had been reasonably lucrative. Americans, unlike the British, appreciated De Saille's entrepreneurial spirit.

However, De Saille reflected, as he removed his

boots and hung them across his saddle; his entrepreneurial spirit might have led him into a business
deal too far.

He looked around at his companions, each standing by their horses, doing their best to stop the
beasts from making any sound. He nodded to Kyle
to signify that he was ready and moved off silently
across the rough ground to the spot where the
posse was camped.

He moved silently and skilfully over the rough
ground quickly taking care to ease his weight on
anything that felt as though it might snap or shift,
so alerting the two men guarding the camp whose
shapes he could see on the low ridge above him.

If De Saille had known the calibre of the guards
he might well have decided to keep his boots on.

Sheriff Coogan had been worried from the start
that the gang would try to make their break after
dark but he knew his men had ridden hard for over
two days and badly needed sleep. He had posted on
watch two of the younger and fitter men, Jobe
Harlson and Bill Brown, the first a clerk at the bank
and the other a farm hand from one of the settle-
ments just outside town. He himself had stayed with
them as long as possible but knew he could no
longer stay awake and had allowed himself a few

precious hours of sleep, leaving them with strict instructions to wake him if they heard any movement from the trapped men.

Coogan had been gone for scarcely fifteen minutes before Harlson slipped off to sleep. Brown tried hard to stay awake but his head kept slipping forward and then jerking back as he fought back to wakefulness.

As De Saille reached the ridge, keeping low to ensure that he was at no time silhouetted against the skyline, he could see at once the state of alertness of the two men.

They were sitting about twenty feet apart, Harlson resting with his back against a rock, while Brown sat on the smallest sharpest rock he could find in an attempt to stay awake.

De Saille drew his gun and moved forward until he was a few feet from Brown.

He then levelled his gun just over Brown's shoulder, pointing straight at Harlson. He held that for a moment, then moved his aim slightly up and fired.

The bullet struck the rock just above Harlson's head, showering him with small pieces, some of which cut and stung his face. He was instantly awake and panicked. Knowing only that the shot must have come from in front of him he raised his rifle and began firing in that direction.

Brown had snapped awake at the sound of the shot and also knew only that someone was firing at him. He immediately raised his rifle and began to return fire. As the two men blazed at each other De Saille dropped down below the level of the ridge.

It helped a certain fatality that both Brown and Harlson were lousy shots but at such close range they could not entirely miss. Brown received a bullet in his upper arm whilst Harlson had a kneecap shattered. Both went down screaming.

A few yards back in the camp men had scrambled awake, grabbing for rifles and handguns. The fastest of them rushed ahead, firing in the direction they believed the outlaws to be. The slowest, knowing that somebody ahead of them was shooting, also began firing.

Coogan was at once trying to maintain order and keep his own head down for there was every danger of it being blown off. He was screaming at the men to cease firing until they knew what the hell it was they were firing at, but he was struggling to make himself heard above the sound of the guns.

Below them, De Saille was swinging himself into the saddle of his horse and following the other men who were already riding as fast as the terrain would allow them, their heads down over their horses.

The madness on the ridge lasted probably no more than a couple of minutes, but when Coogan finally restored order, he had, in addition to Harlson and Brown, one man shot in the hip; another had lost a finger and a third had managed to shoot himself through the foot.

As Coogan sank wearily on to a rock whilst men screamed and sobbed around him he knew that he had let the bank robbers escape from under his nose. He was going to have to return to Tremaine with a shot-up posse and outlaws still every bit at large.

John awoke to thin dawn light with Connie breathing softly beside him. He lay for a moment wondering if he should wake her, talk to her, explain what he was about to do, but he knew that she would try to dissuade him and fetch Josh to dissuade him too, and there was no point as his mind was made up.

He took longer than he had planned to write the note for Josh but he wanted to try and explain.

When he had finished he took his bag with his few belongings and crossed to the livery stable.

As he rode out of Arabella he stopped, and turned for one last look. Although he knew he was doing the right thing he felt sad and confused. He turned up his collar against the slight morning chill and rode towards Abilene.

Two hours later, Josh was awakened by Connie beating on his door. He dragged himself out of bed, pulled on some clothes and opened the door. She passed him in a rush, carrying John's note.

'He's gone Josh, he's gone!'

Josh took the note and put on his glasses, trying to blink the sleep out of his eyes.

Dear Connie and Josh

I am sorry I had to leave without saying goodbye but I thought this way would be easier for everyone.

I have to go back to Canada, back to my regiment and accept whatever punishment is coming to me.

To run was a craven and cowardly act; I have brought shame on the regiment and on my loyal and devoted family.

I will leave the army in disgrace but I will at least have faced my punishment like a soldier of the Queen.

Josh, please believe I have found great pleasure and comfort in your company over these past few weeks and I am proud to consider myself your friend. Please take care of Connie as she may not understand.

Josh avoided the reading the last sentence out loud as Connie was already sobbing fitfully in the corner. He did however read the next part.

And to Connie again I have enjoyed being with you and believe strongly that I am a better person and a richer person for having known you. Please believe in yourself and make a better life for yourself.

You are the very best of people I have ever met and you deserve so much more. You certainly deserve more than a disgraced soldier. Please believe you will be in my thoughts always.

I am forever in the debt of you both. God bless you both,

Your dearest friend,

John.

When Josh finished reading the fitful sobs became full-blown howls of misery. Josh shifted uncomfortably; he had never been able to handle women's tears.

'Don't take on, girl,' was all he could manage. But Connie was determined to 'take on' at full blast.

'Get him back, Josh, get him back,' she managed at last through the wails and cries.

'No,' Josh said firmly.

This quietened Connie a little.

'No . . . this is something he has to do. He got it wrong and now he wants to put it right. Every man has a right to do that.'

'What is the point? They are only going to throw him out of the army. He could stay here and be happy.'

'John is a man of high principle, Connie. He could never be happy with this hanging over him.'

'Do you think he will come back?'

Josh took up his pipe and began to fill it. 'I guess not.'

Josh closed the door on Connie's sobs as he made his way out to the porch.

TEN

Kyle sat in a chair by the window looking down on the streets of Abilene, Kansas. It was late afternoon and already the city was gathering its forces for the loud, bawdy, violent night to come. Kyle liked Abilene. He liked its roaring defiance, its blinkered unfettered delight in getting rich. Abilene was about money and pleasure in equal amounts and those were what Kyle liked to be around.

It had been a hard ride after the five of them had escaped the posse. Whilst he doubted that the Tremaine townsfolk would regroup in time to chase them he had still wanted to put as much distance between him and determined pursuit as possible, so the first two days they had driven the horses hard.

He had made his mind up quickly where he wanted to go. Somewhere they could melt into the crowds and be less visible until the fuss over the events in Missouri died down. They had split up once they reached the city and taken different lodgings, De Saille and Cottin taking one of the good hotels.

One thing Kyle always kept in mind was that whilst Abilene was rough and dangerous, it was far from lawless. Police Chief Tom 'Bear River' Smith controlled the town almost single handed and his reputation was fast growing. Kyle had warned his boys to stay out of trouble and as much as possible, out of sight.

Kyle lit a cigar and let the smoke drift out of the window to where the sounds of music and laughter drifted back.

Music and laughter were in short supply in the hotel room of Andre Cottin. De Saille sat in a window seat surveying a similar scene to Kyle. Cottin had no interest in what was happening outside and was pacing the floor, his arms waving as he spoke.

'I told you not to get involved with these criminals. Now we will be lucky if we are not arrested. If anybody identified us.'

De Saille looked back from the window.

'To identify us, Monsieur Cottin, they would have to have raised their heads higher above those rocks than I saw anybody prepared to do.'

'Nevertheless, I did not come all this way to get involved with a gang of outlaws. I came on a matter of honour that needs to be settled like gentlemen, not to ride with murderers and cuthroats.'

'Your matter of honour will not be settled while there is a US marshal in Arabella. These men give you the opportunity to have your duel, and you will simply have to compromise your high standards with regard to companionship to achieve it.'

De Saille made the last remark pointedly, as it had become clear over the journey north that Cottin considered him an inferior being and was tolerating him only from necessity.

Cottin said nothing but threw himself bad-temperedly into a chair. He knew that De Saille was right and that without the distraction and intervention of these unsavoury men he could not take the revenge on the Englishman that he had promised his family at his brother's funeral.

'How long are we going to be in this ghastly place?'

'Long enough for people to stop chasing after us.'

'It is not us they are chasing after – it is those outlaws.'

112

'At the moment that is the same thing. We will be patient. When the time is right you will have your moment on your "field of honour".'

De Saille did not agree with Cottin's view. He liked Abilene. It was the kind of place where he felt at home, surrounded by gamblers, criminals and whores. For the first time in many days he was beginning to enjoy himself.

John was making his way back from the Abilene rail depot as the noise and bustle of the stockyards flowed around him. After the lazy pace of Arabella the noise and the crowds had come as a shock. However he now had a ticket back East in his pocket, and the determination to go back and put things right. To salvage what could be salvaged and reclaim what little honour there might be in facing up to what he had done.

Lost in thought as he was, he did not notice Wills and Jones approaching from the opposite direction. Indeed so many months had passed since their meeting in The Drover's Rest that it is unlikely he would have remembered them.

They, however, remembered him and Jones pulled Wills sharply back between some cattle pens as he approached.

'It's that English fella.'

'I see him.' Wills was instinctively reaching for his gun but Jones laid a restraining hand on his wrist.

'Not here, Wills, you heard what Kyle said. No trouble here.'

They watched John pass and then quickly made their way towards the hotel.

Kyle did not take the news well. 'What do I have to do,' he asked nobody in particular, 'to get some good fortune here? If that Englishman heads back East, I no longer have De Saille, and I need his gun.'

'You still have us,' Wills reminded him, not a little resentfully.

Kyle looked at him as though he had suggested that strapping a gun on an aggressive racoon might have been a worthy substitute.

Jones had a more practical thought. 'No need for the Frenchies to know.'

Kyle considered this for a moment and shook his head.

'Have you ever seen the way these fellas fight? They don't just ride in with their guns blazing. They meet up first, decide how they're going to do it and arrange a time. Damndest thing you ever saw. Soon as they see he's not there they ride off. No, we've got to get him back to Arabella.'

ELEVEN

It was past midnight and Arabella was largely silent except for the call of animals and the occasional piece of shouted conversation somewhere out there in the dark.

Sheriff Coogan sat staring gloomily out of the window of Josh Ramsey's office at nothing in particular. Jess Coleman poured another cup of coffee, then as an afterthought poured a small measure of whiskey from the bottle that Josh kept at the back of his desk drawer, and handed it to the other man. Coogan sipped gently at the drink.

'It's a damned mess, Jess. Five men wounded – by each other – and that scum halfway to Texas. This is what happens when you have to do a politician's bidding.'

Jess could only silently agree, being here himself

only at the bidding of his own town mayor.

'You certain they are headed south?'

Coogan nodded.

'Couple of the boys tracked them for several miles. They're taking the Chisholm Trail south. Good riddance to them, I say, but I have to go back and tell that horse's ass they've got away. The bastard will have my badge. That's forty dollars a month, a house and pension gone; just because trigger-happy amateurs can't do one good goddamn thing they're told.'

He drained the cup and slammed it down on to the table. 'I've got to go after them, Jess.'

'Don't be a fool, man. Your boys are way out of their league. There will only be more killing.'

'Do you think,' Coogan snorted dismissively, 'that I intend to ride one more mile with that bunch of jittery rabbit hunters? I'm going on my own.'

'Are you crazy? There's five of them.'

'Another man with me, who knew what he was about, would shorten the odds some. Hell Jess, the Englishman is gone and that was all the Frenchies were ever coming here for.'

He looked across at Jess and waited. The marshal played with the ends of his moustache as he always did when wrestling with a problem. He walked to the window and stared out into the night.

'The other two men; you think they were the Frenchmen?'

'One of the boys said he thought the big fella looked like one of the Frenchmen who were in town when the bank was robbed. He thought he heard one of them shout something in French.'

'That's an awful lot of "thinking".'

'Right. And Jethro is not equipped for it, so I do not necessarily pay that much mind, but from what he described could be the same man. Guess they must have been in on the robbery.'

Jess looked unconvinced. 'That doesn't seem to fit with what we've been told. The little guy wants his duel. He is paying the hired gun to make sure it happens. By all accounts money is not his problem. I cannot see one good reason why either of them would want to tie up with a bunch of bank robbers. It just does not figure.'

'Perhaps they thought some extra guns would shorten the odds.'

'Then they are riding in the wrong direction.'

'Perhaps they heard the English fella is headed home. Hell Jess, I don't know. But I do know I cannot go back to Tremaine empty handed. I have to go after them.'

Coogan looked expectantly at Jess yet again.

Jess sighed. 'Well, I would feel a whole lot better knowing those two were on their way back to New Orleans. OK, I'll ride down with you, but I ain't riding out of the territory and neither are you. Once we know they are all well clear of here we ride back to Tremaine and we tell your mayor if he wants those boys so bad he had better get himself on a horse and go look for them. If he tries to take your star I'll tell him he's going to be mayor of a town without a sheriff because I will make damn certain Tremaine gets no support from any marshal in Kansas.'

John sat in the bar listening to cattle men grumbling that the business was dying in Abilene. He found it strangely comforting, like sitting in a London coffee house listening to bankers bemoan the decline of their stocks.

He became aware of the short plump man in an ill-fitting suit watching him from the bar. The man looked nervous; running his fingers round the inside of his collar as if it was choking him, when clearly he could easily insert both his podgy thumbs inside it.

Eventually, as John had suspected he would, the man made his way across the room towards him.

John groaned inwardly, the last thing he wanted at the moment was company. For a moment he hoped he had made a mistake and the man would continue on past his table but he stopped hard by and cleared his throat. 'Would your name be John Carshalton?'

Good manners forced John to his feet. 'You have the advantage of me, sir.'

The nervous man forced a smile, displaying crooked teeth stained brown by tobacco.

'Well, I sure would not want to do that, no, sir. It's just that, well, when I heard you order your drink I could not help overhearing that you was an English fella, and I thought if that man is the English fella I just heard some other fellas talking about then that is a man I need to speak with.'

John felt his stomach tighten. He did not like what he was hearing. With great reluctance, he indicated the empty chair on the other side of the table.

'Will you join me, sir?'

'Well now, that is mighty neighbourly of you.'

The man offered his nicotine stained hand to John.

'Abraham Garnet at your service. Most folks just call me Abe.'

As the whiff of stale tobacco and the result of only

a very occasional meeting with soap and water assailed John's nostrils he suspected that was not all folks called him.

The man sank into a chair and John sat back opposite him. John waited for a few moments but the man noisily slurped his beer and seemed to have forgotten the purpose of his contact.

'You mentioned you had overheard somebody discussing me, Mr Garnet?'

Garnet roused himself and fixed John with another unappealing smile.

'Right, right. Very reason I came over, quite right, quite right.'

He finished his beer and gazed longingly into the empty depths of his glass.

John sighed. 'Can I offer you a drink?'

Garnet brightened on the instant. 'Right neighbourly. Really do not mind if I do. Thank you kindly.'

John signalled to the barman. Garnet chimed in.

'A shot of whiskey would be much appreciated indeed.' John was about to convey this to the barman but he signalled he had heard by reaching for the bottle and a glass. He was watching Garnet with an expression of loathing that suggested a previous acquaintance.

Once Garnet was settled with the glass, and the bottle that he had deftly prised from the barman's grasp, he turned his attention back to the matter in hand.

'Like I was saying, I was down the road at the Stockman's Bar, just minding my own business and passing the time, when I could not help overhearing these fellas talking.'

'Your hearing, sir, seems to be somewhat out of control.'

Garnet blinked vaguely at him. 'Well these fellas . . .'

'Could you describe them?'

'Well, there was a guy with a scar across his face, a young guy without a scar, and older guy, he didn't have no scar either.'

'I think I am cognizant that only one of the party had a scar – go on.'

'And then there was two Frenchies.'

John felt his stomach knot up yet again. 'Frenchmen?'

'Yep . . . big guy and a little neat fella with a moustache. He didn't seem to speak no English but the big fella did. Anyhows they was talking about this English fella, John Carshalton and a place called Arabella, and they was saying that they was heading back down there to finish what they started. Then one of the other fellas said he could swear he had seen John Carshalton here in Abilene and the guy with the scar he ups and says what the hell would you be doing in Abilene? Then the little Frenchie, he sets up shouting something in French and the big fella tells the others that he is calling John Carshalton a coward for running away from a dool, whatever the hell a dool is.'

'That would be a duel.'

'Duel? OK then . . . anyway he was saying that John Carshalton had no honour. So one of 'em says why can't they have the . . . Duel . . . here in Abilene and the man with the scar laughs and says he thinks Tom Smith might just have something to say about that. So all this arguing starts and the guy with the scar says let him run we're heading ourselves down to that stinking little one-whore town and we're going to shoot the living hell out of it. Yes sir that was his words; shoot the living hell out of it. And another of 'em says "Let's ride", and they downs their drinks and takes off out that bar like prairie dogs from a dust storm.'

John was sitting with a sinking heart listening to the repulsive little man relate his tale.

'Now that didn't mean much to me, but when I

heard you order your drink I thought now see here, Abe, it would be one hell of a coincidence but just suppose that English fella there is the same English fella those bad men were talking about. Well, I would not be doing my Christian duty not to tell him what I heard.'

John sighed. 'I am grateful to you, of course. Did they ride out, do you know?'

'Well, I didn't rightly follow them 'cause they was mean-looking men, bad, bad men. But they sure looked as though they were going to.'

John sat for a few moments trying to think. Suddenly he felt his sense of duty was being torn in different directions. In one direction lay duty to his regiment, his family, his Queen. In the other lay duty to his friends and to his honour.

He rose from his chair.

'Allow me to buy you the remains of that bottle for your trouble, Mr Barnet.'

'Well, it was no trouble at all, Mr Carshalton. Just doing my Christian duty, but I won't say as though a nip of the rye doesn't make my old bones feel more rested. That is mighty neighbourly of you, sir.'

John dropped some coins on to the table.

'You going after those bad fellas?'

John simply bowed his head slightly.

'I am much obliged to you, sir.'

With that he left Abe Garnet in the company he liked best.

An hour later Jones was sitting in front of Kyle.

'Abe did as he was bid. The Englishman collected his horse and rode out.'

Kyle relaxed slightly. 'Fine. Pay that stinking little rattlesnake off and tell everyone we are riding out tomorrow.'

TWELVE

On a day that would remain for ever in the minds of those who were there, John stood on the boardwalk outside the Arabella general store in the thin morning light and waited. Two nights before he had ridden back to Arabella and he had unknowingly passed Jess and Coogan somewhere in the darkness.

He had ridden in the following morning and had been greeted by Connie, flinging herself from the saloon and running towards him. By the time he had dismounted she had reached him and rushed against him, pressing her face deep into his chest and wrapping her arms tightly around him.

He managed to reach down and tilt her face upwards towards him. It was already streaked with tears.

'You came back . . . you came back. I thought I would never see you again and you came back to me.'

He said little standing there in the dusty street. He just let her cling to him and enjoy the moment. Eventually he told her he must see Josh and she reluctantly released him. After he had settled his horse in the livery stable he made his way to Josh's office. Josh looked up as he entered and grunted.

'So you're back.'

'So it would seem.'

'Change your mind?'

'Rather I had it changed for me.'

Josh sighed. 'I figured.'

'Did you?'

'Connie thinks you came back for her.'

'And I did, and for you, and for everybody I care about here.'

'You had better tell me.'

So John told him, and Josh listened, sucking on the pipe as he did when he was concentrating. It took only a few minutes for John to relate what had happened but it took a while for Josh to answer.

'John, I've known some clever fellas in my time and you are one of them but I have to declare you are the stupidest clever fella I have ever met.'

'I beg your pardon?'

'And well you might. There you were in Abilene, run by one of the toughest most honest lawmen in the state. Do you go to him and tell him what you heard? Do you get these bank robbing vermin arrested? No, you ride back here so you can carry on with some senseless duel with the Frenchman. Have you got one lick of common sense?'

'Well, Josh, I did not expect you to run into my arms as Connie did, but I had hoped for a better welcome.'

'It's not that I'm not glad to see you, boy, but hell, we have a mess of trouble heading this way. Trouble that could have been avoided if you had just stopped to think instead of jumping on your horse and riding back here as though you were the English cavalry.'

John looked around with sudden concern. 'Where is Jess?'

'You might ask. Jess is off with Sheriff Coogan.'

'Who?'

'Sheriff Cogan is the sheriff of the town whose bank was robbed by the thieving trash we drove out of here. His posse got shot up by that French hired gun. He came here to ask Jess to ride south with him to try and track them down. Just as they was about to leave, a telegram comes from Abilene saying that the whole bunch of them has just shown up there.'

'Then they may have arrived in time to prevent them leaving.'

'We can hope, because if not they are on their way here and now we'll be facing five guns instead of two.'

So it was in low spirits that John returned to the saloon where Connie insisted on preparing breakfast. The food and her welcome company did lift him and later in the day he had decided that all he needed to do was meet the obligation of the duel, and whatever the outcome nothing further would happen.

In any event, he reasoned, Jess and Coogan would have returned by that time and their presence would be more than enough to deter Kyle and his friends.

A flaw in John's reasoning was already being exposed in Abilene, where Jess and Coogan were questioning a panicked Abe Garnet.

'You told Captain Carshalton that those outlaws were headed back to Arabella?'

Jess leaned into Abe's face to underline the aggression in his voice, and then wished that he had not as Abe's fetid breath struck his nostrils.

Abe was sweating profusely which simply increased the unpleasant odour around the man.

'Well, sir, it was like this.'

'Let me tell you what it was like, you piece of mule dung, Kyle Banner paid you to lie to the Englishman to get him to go back to Arabella – why?'

' 'Cause the Frenchie wants his dool.'

'And Kyle wants to shoot three kinds of hell out of the town?'

'Ah. No, sir. No, sirree. It ain't like that at all.'

'What is it like?'

'Kyle and his boys are heading West, sir, yes sir, definitely West, sir.'

Jess exchanged looks with Coogan, who was stroking his moustache and studying Abe with a cynical frown.

'And the Frenchies?'

'Ah well sir, now they are going to Arabella 'cause the little Frenchie wants to have his dool. Kyle says he ain't got no mind to follow no Frenchies on some stupid "dool".'

Coogan leaned forward and like Jess before him quickly leaned back.

'Kyle Banner seems to confide in you a great deal.'

'Oh we have known each other for years, Sheriff Coogan sir. We goes back a long way, does me and Kyle.'

'But your lifelong friendship does not stop you from telling us his plans.'

'I'm only doing my Christian duty, sir.'

Jess reached across and grabbed Abe by the collar.

'You lie to me, you weevil, and I will rip out your lungs and feed them to the prairie dogs.'

The sweat was moving from a stream to a torrent on Abe's face.

'I wouldn't lie, sir, it's like I'm telling it, sir. The Frenchies have gone to Arabella for their dool and Kyle and the boys are heading West. Better pickings West, sir, that's what Kyle, told me. I'm a good Christian, sir.'

'Shut the hell up and get out of my sight.'

He released his grip on Abe, who jumped up, gratefully, rushed for the door, and vanished into the afternoon light.

Jess sat back. 'What do you think?'

'I think if that man told me my name was Coogan and we are sat here in Abilene I would find myself in want of a second opinion.'

'We have to decide, do we believe that reptile and

ride westward or get our asses back to Arabella?'

They sat in silence for a while as the hubbub of the town began to quieten as the sun dropped lower. Eventually Jess stirred.

'It goes against all my instincts to believe that skunk, but he was one frightened man.'

Coogan shrugged. 'Depends who he is most afraid of – Kyle Banner or us.'

'If it was me I would be more afraid of us.'

Jess sighed, 'You could be right. OK, we stop over and get some sleep and then we head West.'

As Jess and Coogan planned their ride west, several miles to the other side of town the two Frenchmen, plus Kyle, Jones and Wills, were sitting by a campfire drinking coffee. They had with them a new member of the crew; a doctor whom Cottin had insisted must be there as part of the etiquette of the duel.

Both Kyle and De Saille had, in forceful terms, condemned the stupidity of this, but the fussy little man would not be dissuaded.

'Where the hell,' Kyle raged, 'does that damned fool think we are going to find a doctor willing to get involved in a venture such a this?'

Abilene however, had a habit of providing just whatever a person could desire, and it provided

Isaiah Peabody.

Isaiah was late of the Confederate army where he had served as a surgeon with the rank of major. Isaiah had, frankly, not been a very good army surgeon and an even worse major. Ex Confederate soldiers spoke of men with appalling injuries crawling across the Union lines to prison and a competent surgeon rather than have Major Peabody operate on them.

On discharge from the army Isaiah had sought solace in drink and found that here at last was something he could do well, and, as with many before him when they find their calling in life, he stuck at it.

Cottin stared aghast at the poorly shaven, shabbily dressed drunk who was paraded before him but as he opened his mouth to protest he was told in no uncertain terms to take it or leave it. He took it.

Now Isaiah huddled on the far side of the fire complaining bitterly about the lack of alcoholic refreshment available, shivering violently as an unaccustomed sobriety began to kick in.

Cottin simply shook his head and pulled the blanket tighter around him. He was, he decided, a civilized man in a nation of barbarians. He found himself wondering if the Englishman was really worth all of this suffering but, as always, convinced himself that honour was everything and that his reputation as a duellist against whom anybody went at their peril would more than compensate for some discomfiture.

He tried to close his ears to Isaiah's pleas and seek blessed sleep.

Further away in Arabella, John was lying with his arms around Connie, enjoying her softness and the silky black hair. She made little murmuring noises of contentment and for the first time in many months John too felt very, very content.

This contentment was to disappear the next day when two things happened. The two lawmen failed to appear and De Saille did.

John had known who it was the moment he saw the big man pull his horse up in from of the saloon. The easy arrogance of manner, the way he moved lightly, almost gracefully for a large man. The streak of cruelty behind the eyes. This man did not belong here, but then, John reasoned; neither did he.

He had stepped down and crossed the street whilst Josh watched, his hand resting lightly on the butt of his revolver. John had caught Josh's eye as he crossed the street and John had tried to give his friend a reassuring smile, but he knew that it only looked as it felt; apologetic.

De Saille offered his hand and John, without hesitating, took it and returned De Saille's short bow. At that Josh shook his head in disgust and turned back into his office.

When De Saille spoke again it was with the weariness of somebody reciting a message they had little interest in.

'I am instructed to ask you if you intend to give Monsieur Andre Cottin satisfaction in the matter of the grave injustice perpetrated against Monsieur Cottin's brother during a duel concerning a grave insult paid to Monsieur Cottin's brother regarding a lady of your mutual acquaintance.' He could not suppress a sigh as he finished his speech.

'As far as I am concerned, sir,' John responded coldly, 'the duel was instigated entirely at the desire of the gentleman's brother and the outcome, although tragic, should be considered to be an end to the matter.'

De Saille wanted to say that he could not possibly agree more, but pressed on. 'Nevertheless, Monsieur Cottin does not agree and asks if you will give him satisfaction in this matter?'

'You may inform Monsieur Cottin that I will indeed meet with him at a time and place of his choosing.'

'He has suggested that we meet here at eight of the clock tomorrow morning. Will that suit?'

'It will.'

'I am asked that you name a friend.'

'I have friends but none that will assist me in this.'

De Saille did not react to this but simply droned on: 'I am also instructed to ask if pistols will be to your liking?'

'Tell him I am pleased to meet him with any weapon he chooses. Pistols will be quite satisfactory.'

'Further, I am to ask if you object to Monsieur Cottin supplying the weapons. He suspects you may not have access to suitable pieces yourself. You will, of course, have first choice of the pieces that are offered.'

John replied stiffly, 'I trust Monsieur Cottin to behave as a man of honour. That will be quite satisfactory.'

De Saille bowed. 'Until tomorrow then.'

John returned the bow and watched De Saille mount his horse and ride away.

As he rode away John started to move towards the sheriff's office but he saw that the door was firmly closed, which was not Josh's custom, so he thought better of it. Later, as he sat alone and brooding in his room, Connie came as she always did.

He was deeply glad and reached as always for the copy of The Pickwick Papers and began to read. She listened for a few moments but with none of the satisfied smiles and spontaneous giggles that were usual. Instead she sat staring at him, her dark eyes full of sadness. Finally she spoke.

'John, please do not.'

He almost instinctively said; 'Do not do what?' but he knew that would be foolish. He knew precisely to what she referred. He laid down the book.

'Connie, I have to.'

'You do not have to. That is foolish. All of this is foolish. You are going to fight a man you hardly know for no more reason than that he has asked you to. You do not even know what it is about any more. Some woman who betrayed you.'

This stung him she knew, but she could not stop now; she pressed on.

'You cannot be unaware of my feelings towards you.' She hesitated but knew she could not stop now. 'I love you, John. I think you are one of the finest and kindest men I have ever met. The times we have spent here have been the happiest of my life.' Tears were beginning to fill her eyes and she angrily forced them back. 'I know you do not feel the same towards me, but I cannot believe you do not feel some regard for me, and I am very content to settle for that. I could be such a good companion to you, John. I could look after you if only you would let me.'

His mind was in turmoil. He had expected none of this and did not know how to respond. He wanted to reach for her, but instead he simply said 'Connie.'

But she raised her hand to stop him. 'Hear me out. When that man comes tomorrow, you tell him that you are not going to join in this madness. You tell him to turn and ride away and to take his hired gun with him. Deputy Ramsey will stand beside you and so will all of this town, because they are your friends.'

'Connie, I cannot do that.'

'Why? In the name of heaven, why? If you cared anything for your friends, anything at all for me.'

'It is a matter of honour.'

'John, we are in America. We are not in Europe where foolishness like this is important. I have made this country my home. It is a new world, John, full of new ideas. Not the tired, washed-out, dying animal that Britain has become.'

This was not the thing to say to a man who had worn the British Army uniform with pride.

John rose stiffly to his feet. 'I was proud to serve my queen and my country, and I would be proud to do so again. I happen to believe in the values of that "washed out" country. Many a despot has thought us "washed out", and learned of their miscalculation to their cost. As far as America is concerned I have seen nothing in my journeys here other than cut-throats, liars and thieves and if that is what you hold dear than I wish you joy of it, madam.'

Connie looked for a moment as though she had been slapped.

'Madam? Did you just call me madam?'

She clenched her small fists and advanced on John who in turn took an involuntary step backwards.

'Madam? My name is Connie, the name you call out in your passion, the name you speak with such tenderness when it is just the two of us together.'

For a moment her voice caught, but then her anger steadied it. 'You pompous, arrogant English snob. You care more for your honour, for your uniform and your damned queen. Well, sir, I wish you joy of them because you clearly have no further use for me.' With that, she turned and stormed from the room.

In that moment he wanted to run after her, to throw his arms around her and beg her to stay. Instead he simply sat on his cot, feeling more alone than he had ever felt in his life.

Now as he stood dressed in his army uniform and waited, he saw three figures on horseback appear at the end of the main street riding slowly towards him. He knew that there was still time to stop this. Time to stop it at no cost. The people of the town would see it only as a victory for common sense.

But the sense of duty, the values with which he had been raised, the importance of honour to a soldier of the Queen. These were not things he could betray.

He watched as the riders got closer. At first he thought they had brought one of the outlaws with them, but realized he did not recognize the third man, who was shabby, unkempt and pallid.

He vaguely remembered Cottin, who looked depressingly like his unpleasant brother.

The three men dismounted.

Josh had stepped out on to the sidewalk and was

watching the three intently. He was in an agony of indecision. He deeply regretted that he had not intervened the previous evening. Then would have been the time to arrest De Saille for, well, almost anything, so long as it forced an end to this stupidity. However, he had not. Instead he had sulked in his office and allowed the arrangements to be made. He could not stop this now without humiliating his friend. At least, he reasoned, there appeared to be no sign of Kyle Banner and the others.

Connie appeared beside Josh. Her eyes were red rimmed from crying and it was obvious she had had no sleep, but then he thought grimly, who had?

'Stop them, Josh,' Connie said simply.

'Damn it, Connie, I cannot.'

She turned away. 'Damn you, then! Damn all men for their arrogance and their foolishness.'

She had thought herself cried out but more tears came.

Cottin and De Saille approached John. Cottin bowed stiffly and spoke in French. De Saille translated.

'Monsieur Cottin inquires if you are well.'

John returned the bow.

'Very well, thank you.'

Josh shook his head. Not for the first time he decided that all Europeans were crazy, but the craziest of all were the French and the English.

Cottin spoke again, indicating the shambling creature standing a few feet behind them. De Saille smiled faintly.

'Monsieur Cottin would like me to name Dr Isaiah Peabody who will attend to any wounds.'

John studied the filthy unshaven man and shook his head. 'We must only pray that any hit is fatal.'

De Saille did not bother to translate this. Peabody was beyond caring about insults. Every nerve end in his body hurt and, coward though he was, he knew with certainty that he would fight any man for a sip of whiskey.

'Are you ready?' De Saille asked coldly and simply.

John spoke loudly enough for Connie and Josh to hear.

'I have been a party to no quarrel with the gentleman that I am aware of. The tragic events concerning his brother were the result of that gentleman's challenge to me. In all possible circumstances, the matter should be considered to be resolved. I ask the gentleman to think again

141

before embarking on this course of action.'

De Saille translated this to Cottin. Cottin muttered angrily to De Saille.

As he spoke, John stared hard at the small Frenchman. He noted that the cool assurance he had seen before in Canada had gone. Instead there was agitation and discomfiture.

De Saille turned back. 'He says that you forced his brother into a duel he could not win. You therefore behaved dishonourably. If you wish to retire from the field you can do so but you will be without honour and can no longer be considered a gentleman.'

John looked around him at the main street of the dusty little Plains township. Retire from the field! he thought, and realized for the first time how incongruous it seemed to be observing these old world courtesies in this utterly inappropriate place.

'Proceed,' he said wearily.

De Saille took down a slim wooden case that was hanging from his saddle. He opened it to reveal two flintlock duelling pistols which John had to concede were ornate and beautifully crafted. They were made, he read on the case, by Wogden and Barton of London.

De Saille offered the guns to John for his inspection. John, as he was expected to do, examined the barrels to ensure they were smooth-bore not rifled, which would have been considered extremely bad form.

He nodded and handed the pistols back to De Saille, who began the process of loading; adding just the right amount of black powder, wrapping the ball in a cloth and ramming it down into the barrel with the small rod provided.

While this was happening, John glanced down the street to where the stagecoach had been halted by Josh some time before. He could see that the driver was still on the box seat with his foot causally resting against the brake.

When the stage had arrived an hour earlier, Josh had stopped it further up the street than was normal explaining the reason why to Frank Tracy, the elderly driver. The stage had two passengers that morning; a lace salesman from Chicago, busily selling his stock to respectable lady and whore alike in every cattle town he came to. The other was a gambler who took one look at the lean pickings of Arabella and decided to keep moving.

At Frank's recommendation, they had both repaired to Widow Brady's boarding house to enjoy a breakfast of ham and eggs. Normally Frank would have joined them but, on being told that a

Frenchman and an Englishman were about to shoot each other with antique pistols, he had decided to stay and enjoy the show.

He was so engrossed in the spectacle unfolding in front of him that he took a moment to realize that there was a man standing down beside the stage, with a pistol pointed up at his head.

Kyle smiled up at him.

'I would be grateful, sir, if you would climb down and join myself and my business associates.'

Josh, like everybody else, was intent on the duel. Frank could have shouted for help but Kyle looked like a man who meant business. He climbed down. Kyle led him to the back of the stagecoach where Jones and Wills were waiting with pistols drawn. Kyle rested the barrel of his pistol against Frank's head.

'Nobody needs to get hurt, ol' timer. All you need to do is get up there and quietly and without fuss hand down the box that has the army payroll in it.'

Frank stared uncomprehendingly at him.

'The what that has the what?'

'We can do this hard or easy, old man. I just want the box that has the seventy-five thousand dollars of soldiers' pay.'

Frank forgot his initial fear and spat a stream of

tobacco juice into the dust.

'Son, do you think that if I had seventy-five thousand dollars riding behind me I would not turn this rig south and not stop till I was over the border sitting in some cantina with a *señorita* on my arm and a good bottle in my hand?' He shook his head and let out a cackle.

'Seventy-five thousand dollars! That is a good one; yes, sir, that is just the drollest thing I have ever heard.' He cackled again.

Kyle grabbed Frank by his shirt collar. 'Then why, you lying son of a bitch, do you have two men riding shotgun all the way down here?'

'I have not had a man riding shotgun with me since the Indians quieted down. All I have for company are the prairie dogs and my own farts.'

'You have soldiers come here to meet the stage.'

'Only when I have some officer and his wife. Then they send out a rig from the fort.'

Kyle felt a sinking feeling in the pit of his stomach. He could not bring himself to look at Jones and Wills. Instead he climbed up the back of the stage and began opening the boxes. He opened two before a storm of lace blew into his face and he knew with a terrible certainty that he had been lied to. For all his experience, for all the years he had robbed and harmed, he had been duped because he had wanted to believe it, to believe that here was his way out, his ticket to California and a comfortable old age. He tore at pieces of lace in his rage.

Back down the street, John and Cottin had taken their pistols and were standing back to back. Both pistols were half-cocked.

'At my command you will both step twenty paces, turn, and fire in your own time. There will be one shot only, after which the matter must be considered to be resolved.'

John began to step forward. As he did he decided that he would not shoot to kill. Instead he would fire wide; deloping as it was known. He knew how this practice was frowned upon, indeed banned by Code Duello but he no longer cared. Frankly, enough was enough. Cottin would not delope and if Cottin killed him, then so be it, but he would no longer be a party to this stupidity.

He now knew, too late, what really mattered to him, and that was Connie. He knew with a dreadful certainty that he loved her and he would not get the chance to tell her.

The scream from Connie cut across these thoughts. He turned and it was this that saved his life, for as he turned, the ball from Cottin's pistol tore off his right earlobe and nicked the side of his neck.

The pain for a moment was excruciating, and he swayed as his eyes watered. He shook his head to clear it and saw Cottin standing only a few yards in front of him with the smoking pistol in his hand, staring in horror at John.

John for a moment could not comprehend what he was seeing, then a terrible anger rose inside him. It had all been about honour. From the first sense-less duel that had robbed him of his job and his woman, to his agreeing to risk his new happiness in this small Western town. In the end, he had risked it all for a man with no honour at all.

He raised his pistol and pointed it at Cottin. He did not know in that moment if he was actually going to pull the trigger but he never found out.

Cottin's legs buckled and he fell to knees in the middle of the dusty street babbling at John in French. John understood none of it but knew that Cottin was pleading for his life. He relaxed his finger on the trigger because he knew that there was no way he could shoot the terrified man. He knew also that there was no need. Cottin was pub-licly disgraced; he would no longer issue challenges of any kind.

The second cry of warning a few seconds later came from Josh. Again instinct saved John. He swung his head right to see De Saille starting to draw his gun.

De Saille had had enough. He had tolerated this ridiculous little man for the money that he would earn. Those earnings had looked more promising with the chance of a share of stolen army payroll. The one thing he had always assumed was that Cottin would at least fight his nonsense duel. Now he was blubbering in the middle of the street. The diversion which should have resulted in somebody dying was over. Now it was down to him to give Kyle time to find the payroll.

As John turned and realized what was happening his arm came up straight, the pistol pointing directly at De Saille. He pulled the trigger. There was the momentary pause common with flintlock pistols, then the gun fired. At such close range the ball drilled itself into De Saille's forehead. The force of the shot pushed him backwards so that his shoulder blades crashed against the door frame of the general store. De Saille stood for a moment with a puzzled look on his face, then sank to his knees. He rocked backwards and forwards for a moment until his brain registered that he was dead. Then he folded backwards on to his ankles and lay still.

It was at this point that accounts of the order in which things occurred differed from one observer to another; the truth is it happened this way:

Kyle, busy on top of the stage, looked up at the sound of the two pistol shots and hauled himself forward over the boxes and trunks. There the sight that met his eyes confirmed that everything had gone horribly, terribly wrong.

De Saille was clearly dead on the sidewalk, the small Frenchman was kneeling and blubbering in the centre of the street, and the Englishman had the smoking duelling pistol in his hand. Kyle lost whatever composure he had managed to keep and made the instant decision that if he was going to leave this town empty-handed, he was going to leave an Englishman and a deputy sheriff dead, and indeed, anybody else who cared to get in his way. He was already wanted for murder after the shooting in Tremaine and he might as well leave two more corpses before he and the boys headed south towards Mexico. With this in his mind, he levelled his pistol at John Carshalton and fired.

The shot kicked up the dirt next to John's feet. He swung to face the direction of the shot and at the same time threw himself to his right towards the sidewalk. His fingers closed around De Saille's discarded revolver as Kyle's second shot tore a sliver of wood from a timber upright. It ripped John's cheek, adding more blood to that flowing from his injured ear.

At that moment, Jess and Coogan appeared at the far end of Main Street, coming at full gallop.

The two lawmen had ridden ten miles out of Abilene heading west without uttering a word until Jess had reined in his horse turned to Coogan and said simply, 'We have been lied to. And like two virgins at a church social, we have lifted up our skirts.'

Without a word, Coogan nodded his agreement and wheeled his horse about.

Two hours later, they were again in the company of one Abe Garnet, only this time neither lawman was in the humour for protracted discussion. Jess had his pistol pressed to Abe's groin and explained, before Abe wasted his time confirming his good Christian credentials, that his next visit to a place of worship would be without a treasured part of his anatomy. At this the stench from Abe became overpowering, but they survived it long enough for Abe to update them on the real whereabouts of Kyle and the boys and the reason why they were there.

As Coogan and Jess rode out of Abilene Coogan asked, puzzled, 'They send the army payroll on the back of the stage?'

'First I've heard of it,' Jess responded. Then leaning low over his horse's neck, he drove hard towards Arabella.

Now, their horses drenched in sweat and almost spent, they rode at full gallop down the main street.

Kyle was momentarily distracted by the appearance of the two riders and glanced back. John took this opportunity to move forward, not firing until he was in better range. Then, as Kyle turned back and levelled his pistol again at the approaching Englishman, John dropped to one knee. As Kyle's shots kicked up the dust beside him, he aimed up at the outlaw and fired three times. Two shots caught Kyle in the chest, the other went high and hit him in the throat. Kyle was rocked back by the shots, then he pitched forward over the driver's box and on to the traces of the stage. The horses, already terrified by the shooting, panicked when Kyle's body landed amongst them and reared up as far as the traces would allow.

By this time, Jess and Coogan were almost upon the other outlaws at the back of the stage. Frank, at the sight of the approaching horsemen fell to the ground and crawled under the stage. Jess and Coogan both had guns drawn. Coogan, as an ex-cavalry officer, knew the difficulties of firing from horseback. Jess was just finding out.

Jess began firing first as they bore down on Wills and Jones. Both men had their guns out and were returning the fire. Coogan waited until he was almost on top of the gunmen before he fired.

The terrified team of horses in front of the stage-coach twisted themselves sideways, snapping the doubletree between the leaders and the near-wheel-ers, so that the leaders slewed out in front of the two lawmen.

Coogan fired as he came level with the two men and the exchange of fire was at close quarters. The result was that Jess was hit in the back as he rode past and Jones was hit twice in the stomach. A shot also tore flesh off the rump of Coogan's horse. Crazed with pain, it lurched left and collided with the two panicked horses still yoked together. The collision had two results, one being that Coogan swerved into the wounded Jess, who was thrown from his horse, while Coogan's horse went down. Coogan remembered his training and kicked himself clear but unfortunately, the horse kept rolling straight over the top of him. The second result was that the two lead horses were deflected straight at the kneeling Cottin, who was still wailing, oblivious to what was going on around him. The team went straight over him. He managed a single shrill scream before he was flung about like tumbleweed beneath the hoofs of the horses. They plunged on, leaving him crumpled and still in the dust. The team galloped off down Main Street.

Behind the stage, Jones was on his back, clutching his stomach, groaning and whimpering with the pain. Wills took one panicked look at him, grabbed up the other man's gun and ran across Main Street, firing both revolvers as he went. Josh, on the far side of the street, pushed Connie to the boardwalk and returned the fire.

Wills passed within yards of the deputy sheriff and John, still kneeling in the dust, could only marvel that neither of them appeared to have been hit. Wills disappeared down a side alley and with a terse 'stay there' to Connie, Josh ran, as fast as aching limbs would allow, down the alley after him.

Behind the buildings was a dry creek. Josh nearly stumbled down it. He checked for a moment, expecting fire from the young outlaw, and then saw him standing on a small narrow bridge over the creek, swaying slightly.

153

'Just drop your guns very slow, son.'

Slowly, Wills turned towards Josh, his guns still in his hands, but they were hanging at his sides. Josh felt his fingers tightening on the trigger of his own gun, but then he saw the dark-red stain down the front of Wills's blouse.

Wills was staring at him with a confused and pleading expression on his face, then his legs sagged and he pitched down into the dry creek.

Josh slid gingerly down into the creek beside Wills, who looked at him with pleading eyes.

'I think you've killed me.'

Bubbles of blood were forming on the young man's lips. Josh had seen enough men dying to know that he was looking at another one.

'There's a doctor back there, son, I'll fetch him.'

'Will he stop me from dying?'

'I reckon he'll do his best.'

'I don't really want to die. We were supposed to get rich and instead I'm dying.'

'I won't be a minute, son.'

Josh had just turned to climb out of the creek when Wills suddenly cried out at the top of his voice.

'I'm sorry, Pa, I'm real sorry, it won't happen. . . .'

There was a dreadful rattle in the young man's

lungs such as Josh had heard so often and blood spilled out of Wills's mouth. He jerked for a few moments and then was still.

Josh sat down on the dusty slope of the creek staring at the dead boy. He took off his hat, ran his fingers through what was left of his hair and tears began to run silent and uninterrupted down his face.

Back in Main Street, the period of unreal silence that had followed Josh's disappearance down the alley was broken by what sounded like a hundred voices calling and many feet running.

The good Dr Peabody was standing on the sidewalk, a man in a daze. He could not remember that, even in his worse delirium tremor, he had ever seen anything as strange and horrible as that which he had just witnessed. He was trying to convince himself that he would at any moment awaken in his filthy but familiar cot, when Connie appeared in front of him.

'Help them,' she demanded.

'Help?' he said vaguely, 'Help who?'

'Them,' Connie shouted, casting her arm about to indicate the street. 'Help them.'

Peabody still looked bewildered, so Connie, who knew a drunk when she saw one, struck him hard across the face.

Peabody staggered for a moment, then shook his head to clear it, grabbed up his bag and walked unsteadily into the street.

Somebody, doubting the doctor's healing powers, was already riding towards the fort to enlist the services of the army surgeon.

It must be said that the people of Arabella showed more compassion than had those of Tremaine. Regardless of who these people were they set about trying to give what aid they could, whilst Peabody, whether through the natural instinct of his calling, or fear of Connie hitting him again, found a clarity he had not enjoyed for some time and was doing his best to mend the broken.

Jones had been shot in the stomach and there was little Peabody could do. Several of the womenfolk administered what comfort they could and Jones would linger for several hours before slipping into a coma from which he would not wake.

Jess had been shot in the shoulder and the bullet was lodged in him. Peabody wisely decided to wait for the army surgeon to remove it. This the man successfully did, and fortunately, it being his left shoulder, the resulting permanent stiffness would not greatly affect his work. Coogan had broken his leg when his horse had rolled over him, and Peabody successfully set it. Coogan would limp for the rest of his life, but his personal standing in Tremaine would increase enormously.

Cottin, who, everybody was amazed to find, was still alive, was of greater concern. Peabody decided not to move him until the army surgeon arrived. So he was covered with blankets and shielded from the sun, and lay making odd little moaning sounds. It would be found that his many broken bones included some in his back; he would never walk again. He spent the rest of his life in a wheelchair and after initially trying to blame his position on a cowardly attack by John Carshalton, which nobody believed, and was further discredited by reports filtering north from the USA. He decided to withdraw from society and live out his days as a recluse.

Kyle and Jones would be buried in unmarked graves and soon forgotten. Wills's body would be claimed and collected several days later by an elderly couple; a small grim-faced man who said little, and a plump woman who had cried all she could cry and simply looked empty and lonely.

John had found himself wandering through this madness feeling slightly weak and hurting down one side of his face.

Connie had taken him firmly by his hand and sat him down on the step in front of the jail. There she began to administer to his wounds, slapping his hand away if he tried to protest against painful intrusion. Part way through providing this first aid she threw her arms around him, kissing him hard on the mouth, then she returned to her ministrations as though nothing had happened.

'I will go back,' John told her.

'Whatever you think is correct.'

'I love you and I want you to come with me.'

She paused for a moment at that, bit hard on her bottom lip, then continued applying a bandage around his torn ear.

'Connie, I love you,' he said again, believing she had not heard him.

'I know that,' she said harshly, then softer, 'women always know before men do.'

John was vaguely aware that Josh had emerged from the alleyway down which he had last seen him chasing after Wills. He was also vaguely aware that Josh was not wearing his gunbelt.

Josh surveyed the scene on Main Street, then walked over to where Connie was bandaging John. He looked inquiringly at her and she nodded to confirm that all was well.

Josh took the tin star from his vest and dropped it on the sidewalk between John and Connie, then he turned and walked away.

Both of them looked at the star for a few moments. Neither said anything, then they looked back at each other and Connie continued to apply the bandage.